Georgina's ga
amused one.

It was far too soon
experiencing moments of enforced in
Andrew—in fact, that was the one thing she had
been hoping to avoid at all costs. It was just unfortunate that in those first few moments of her new
job they should have been drawn together on a
case involving a child, a little girl who, with her
long fair hair, bore a striking resemblance to their
daughter Lauren, or rather how Lauren had been
a few years ago—in happier times.

Laura MacDonald lives in the Isle of Wight and is married with a grown-up family. She has enjoyed writing fiction since she was a child, but for several years she worked for members of the medical profession, both in pharmacy and in general practice. Her daughter is a nurse and has helped with the research for Laura's medical stories.

Recent titles by the same author:

WINNING THROUGH
POWERS OF PERSUASION
DRASTIC MEASURES

TO HAVE AND TO HOLD

BY
LAURA MACDONALD

MILLS & BOON®

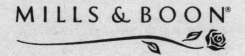

*MILLS & BOON and MILLS & BOON with the Rose Device
are registered trademarks of the publisher.*

*First published in Great Britain 1998
Harlequin Mills & Boon Limited,
Eton House, 18-24 Paradise Road, Richmond, Surrey TW9 1SR*

© Laura MacDonald 1997

ISBN 0 263 80517 4

*Set in Times 10 on 11 pt. by
Rowland Phototypesetting Limited
Bury St Edmunds, Suffolk*

03-9801-50569-D

*Printed and bound in Great Britain
by Mackays of Chatham PLC, Chatham*

CHAPTER ONE

'DADDY'S got a girlfriend,' said Natasha as she climbed into the car.

'Really?' Georgina hoped she sounded noncommittal. 'What's she like?'

'She's all right, I s'ppose.' Natasha wrinkled her nose.

'Well, I didn't like her,' said Lauren flatly. 'I think she's silly and far too young for Dad.'

Georgina swallowed. 'How old is she?'

'Oh, really young,' said Natasha, fastening her seat belt, 'and dead trendy—she wears leggings just like us.'

Georgina digested this piece of information in silence. Really, it was no concern of hers now who Andrew got himself mixed up with, not unless it involved the girls. Then, of course, it would become her concern.

'Dad said could you wait a moment?' said Lauren. 'He had to answer the phone.'

'Does he want to see me?' Georgina rested her hands on the steering-wheel and glanced up the pathway to Andrew's flat.

'Yes,' said Lauren, 'about next weekend, I think.'

'You're with me next weekend.' Georgina spoke more sharply than she had intended.

'He knows that,' said Lauren, 'but he still wants to see you.'

'We had a really good time today,' said Natasha after a moment. 'Daddy took us to the ice rink.'

'It would have been better without her—Denise,' said Lauren with a sniff.

'Is that her name?' Georgina glanced in her driving mirror, her eyes meeting those of her elder daughter.

Lauren nodded. 'Yes, Denise White,' she said.

At that moment Andrew appeared in the doorway of the flat and ran down the path to the car. Georgina's heart gave the same old familiar lurch that it always gave whenever she caught sight of her ex-husband. She should have got over all that by now, she knew that, but somehow she doubted she ever would get over Andrew Merrick completely.

She wound down her window and the chill December air hit her cheeks.

'Hello.' He smiled, the same lazy, heavy-lidded smile she knew so well.

'Andrew.' She inclined her head slightly. 'You wanted to see me?' As she spoke she glanced up at the flat. No doubt the girlfriend was watching, was even now standing behind the curtains to catch a glimpse of her to see what she looked like.

'Yes. It was about next weekend.' Andrew leaned on the frame of the open window and grinned at the girls. 'Oh, I know it's your turn,' he said when he caught sight of her expression, 'but my mother's coming to the Island for the weekend and rather wanted to see the girls.'

'Grandma's coming?' squeaked Natasha from the back seat. 'Oh, can we see her? Please, Mummy, can we?'

Georgina only hesitated for a moment. She was fond of Andrew's mother and knew that the girls adored her. 'Yes,' she said, 'yes, of course. But it had better be the Sunday—they're booked for a riding lesson on the Saturday.' She looked up at Andrew.

'That's fine. No problem. Can't have you missing that, can we?' Andrew smiled at the girls again and then, turning his attention back to Georgina, he said, 'I'll pick them up around ten o'clock.'

She nodded and he moved back and straightened up, but when she attempted to wind up the window he bent forward again and said, 'Everything all right, Georgina?'

She stiffened. 'Yes, everything is fine,' she said crisply.

'I thought you were looking a bit peaky.'

'I'm perfectly all right, thank you,' she said, winding the window right up.

'Bye, Daddy.' The girls waved as she drew smartly away from the kerb.

She looked once in her driving mirror and saw Andrew standing on the pavement, watching them. She swallowed. I bet he doesn't tell his girlfriend she's looking peaky, she thought with a sudden rush of irritation. But, then, he quite obviously hadn't known this girl for long, certainly not as long as the sixteen years he'd known her, Georgina. Because that's what it was. Sixteen years since he'd first come to the Isle of Wight and taken over her life.

'We had fish and chips for lunch.' Natasha was talking again and Georgina forced herself to concentrate on what her daughter was saying.

Twenty minutes later they arrived at Newtown and pulled up before the tiny whitewashed cottage that Georgina had bought following the divorce.

The girls immediately unfastened their seat belts and scrambled from the car, but Georgina sat for a moment and gazed up at the cottage. In the summer months it was quite beautiful, with wisteria climbing the walls and with the borders packed with delphiniums, azaleas and roses. Now, in the middle of winter, it looked bleak and rather forlorn.

Georgina was a summer person. She loved the feel of warm sun on her shoulders, the scent of flowers and the drone of bees. She pined and fretted in the damp chill of winter and longed for warmth and blue skies.

With a sigh she switched off the engine and was about to get out of the car when she heard the sound of another vehicle. Looking in her mirror, she saw that a car had drawn up behind her and a woman was getting out.

For one moment Georgina didn't recognise her visitor but as she got out of her own car, locked the door and turned she exclaimed with delight. 'Why, it's Helen!' she exclaimed. 'How lovely to see you.'

'Hello, Georgie, long time no see. How are you?'

'I'm well. Very well. But what brings you out here to Newtown?' Georgina knew that Helen Turner lived at Gatcombe, several miles away.

'I was wondering if you could spare me a few minutes,' said Helen.

'Of course. Come in and have a cup of tea,' said Georgina quickly. 'Let me just sort the girls out. They've been with Andrew for the weekend. . .but I dare say you already know that.'

'I'm not sure whether Andrew mentioned it or not,' replied Helen as she followed Georgina up the path to the front door, where Lauren and Natasha were waiting on the step.

'Girls,' said Georgina, 'look who's come to see us. You remember Miss Turner, don't you?'

'Oh, Helen, please,' Helen Turner protested. 'Hello, Lauren, Natasha. Goodness, you've grown so much I would hardly have recognised you. Are you still riding these days?'

'Yes.' Lauren smiled. 'I'm learning dressage now.'

'You work at the hospital, don't you?' said Natasha, who had been staring intently at their visitor as if trying to remember who she was.

'Yes. For my sins.' Helen Turner laughed and glanced at Georgina, who had closed the front door and followed them into the cosy sitting-room.

'With Daddy.' Natasha obviously hadn't finished. 'You work in Casualty with Daddy.'

'Lauren,' said Georgina, 'would you go and put the kettle on for tea, please, and, Natasha, would you go and feed the animals? Helen wants to talk to me.'

'Do I have to?' Natasha looked with interest from her mother to Helen. 'I'd rather stay.'

'I dare say you would,' replied Georgina, 'but I want you to go and feed the animals.'

Natasha pouted and Helen quickly intervened. 'What animals have you got?' she asked.

'A rabbit, two guinea pigs and a gerbil,' said Natasha.

'Well, you go and feed them and after I've finished talking to Mummy I would like to come and see them, if that's all right with you.'

'Course it is,' said Natasha, following her sister out of the room.

Georgina smiled and shut the door behind her. 'She's an inquisitive little animal, that one,' she said. 'Always afraid she's going to miss something.'

'Which means, no doubt, she'll be back very soon so I'll get on with what I wanted to say,' said Helen with a laugh.

'Well, please sit down.' Georgina indicated the chintz-covered sofa, and when Helen had settled herself in one corner she sat opposite her in her old-fashioned rocking-chair. 'You've got me really intrigued now.' Her eyes suddenly narrowed. 'This doesn't have anything to do with Andrew, does it?'

'No,' Helen replied. 'At least,' she added, 'not directly.' She paused and when Georgina remained silent she shot her a look. 'I was wondering,' she went on after a moment, 'if you were still interested in returning to work?'

'Well, yes. Yes, I am.' Georgina nodded.

'There's a staff nurse post going on the unit,' said Helen.

Georgina stared at her. 'You mean on Accident and Emergency?'

'Yes, your old job, in fact. It would be perfect for you, Georgie.'

'I've been away from nursing for a long time now. . .'

'There are refresher courses. . .'

'Yes. . .but. . .'

'But what?' Helen was watching her closely.

'It would mean working with Andrew.'

'Yes, I know. Would that bother you?'

'I don't know.' Abruptly Georgina stood up and turned to the window. 'I'm not sure.'

'You two used to work together,' said Helen quietly.

'That was before,' Georgina said sharply, 'before—' She broke off.

'I've aways been under the impression that you two had a very amicable sort of arrangement,' said Helen after a moment's silence.

'I'm not sure I'd go that far,' said Georgina, 'more civilised than amicable. . .and it hasn't always been that. . . At one time it was pretty bloody, I can tell you. . .'

'Yes, I suppose it was,' Helen agreed then added, 'How long is it now since the divorce?'

'Two years.'

'As long as that?' She looked amazed. 'How time flies.'

'Actually, I have applied for one or two jobs just recently.'

'Really? What sort of jobs?' Helen looked surprised.

'School helper was one—because I thought the hours and holidays would be right to fit in with the girls. Trouble was, about a hundred other mothers had the same idea.' Georgina gave a short laugh. 'Then I applied for practice nurse at the Fleetwood Medical Centre but I think they wanted someone with fewer ties than me. . . Oh, and, believe it or not, I very nearly applied for a job at the Shalbrooke.'

'The hospital? Which department?' asked Helen with interest.

'Gynae.'

'So why didn't you?'

'The hours were wrong. It involved some nights and most weekends.'

'Well, I think you'd find the flexible shifts on A and E would suit you down to the ground.'

'I don't know, Helen. . .' Still Georgina looked dubious.

'You were prepared to go for Gynae. ...'

'Yes, but Andrew's not on Gynae,' she protested.

'So, are you saying that's the only reason that would stop you?'

'No. Yes. Probably. Oh, I don't know, Helen. I'm not sure. I just don't think it would be a very good idea, that's all. . .' She broke off as the door was flung open and Natasha bounced back into the room.

'Have you finished talking?' she demanded then, looking at Helen, she said, 'Would you like to come and see the animals now?'

'Why not?' Helen stood up just as Lauren appeared in the open doorway.

'I've made the tea,' she said.

'Well done,' said Georgina. 'It can stand while Helen sees the animals.'

'Maybe by then you will have come to a decision,' said Helen.

Natasha looked up quickly. 'What about?' she said.

'About whether or not your mum should apply for a job on A and E,' Helen replied.

'That's Dad's unit,' said Lauren from the doorway.

'Exactly,' replied Georgina drily.

'That would be absolutely brilliant,' said Natasha, looking wide-eyed from one to the other. 'Mummy and

Daddy working together—wouldn't it, Laurie?' She turned excitedly to her sister.

'Yes. . .' Lauren nodded, then glanced anxiously at Georgina. 'At least I think it would. . . What do you think, Mum?'

'I'm not sure,' replied Georgina. 'I'd need to think about it.'

'Fine,' said Helen as Natasha, dancing ahead, led the way outside to a small outbuilding at the rear of the cottage which housed the children's pets. 'But don't take too long. There will be plenty of others after the job and I would dearly love to have you on my team. . .' She trailed off as Natasha opened a hutch and took out a long-haired guinea pig. 'What a handsome little chap,' Helen said admiringly. 'What's his name?'

'Actually, he's a she,' said Natasha, 'and her name is Annabel.'

'Hello, Annabel,' Helen dutifully took the little animal and admired the rest of the girls' menagerie. 'Lovely animals,' she said at last. 'And you keep them very well, too,' she added, glancing round the outhouse.

'I would like a pony, really,' said Lauren.

'That would make it a bit cramped in here,' said Helen tactfully.

'We wouldn't keep it in *here*,' said Natasha incredulously. 'If we had a pony it would have to be stabled and have a paddock to run in.'

'Finances won't run to that, I'm afraid,' said Georgina as they went back into the house. 'Oh, things aren't too bad,' she added, catching sight of Helen's raised eyebrows. 'Andrew's very good really with maintenance but, what with two mortgages to pay and the girls getting older, everything just gets so expensive. . .'

'All the more reason for getting back to your career.'

'Yes, I suppose so. . .but. . .' Georgina still sounded doubtful.

While the girls disappeared upstairs to their bedroom to change she poured the tea and carried it through to the sitting-room again.

'The money isn't brilliant, but it's much better than it used to be,' said Helen as she took the cup and saucer from Georgina and sat down again.

'I doubt it would buy a pony,' replied Georgina drily.

'Probably not,' agreed Helen, 'but it would help with the riding lessons and school trips and things like that. . .'

'That's true.' Thoughtfully Georgina sipped her tea.

'And, let's face it, why should you go and work in a school or somewhere else when you are a fully trained staff nurse? Besides, I tell you, Georgie, I need you. I never quite got over the fact that you didn't come back after Natasha was born.'

'I had intended to. . .but, well, Andrew had qualified by then and we weren't so desperate for the money as we had been when Lauren was born. . . We were as poor as church mice then. . . But, well, after Natasha things changed. Andrew wasn't so keen on me going back to work then. . .' She set her cup and saucer down on a small coffee-table.

'But what about you—what did you want?' asked Helen.

'Oh, I always intended to resume my career, but I agreed to put it on hold until Natasha started school. . . But then, after what happened—after the divorce—I guess I sort of lost interest and, besides, I felt I should be here at home for the girls. . . They'd had enough trauma, without me flitting off to work. . .'

'You're probably right,' Helen nodded, 'but, surely, now. . .?'

'Yes, it's different now and, like I said, I have been applying for jobs. . .' Helplessly Georgina trailed off and they sipped their tea in silence.

After a moment Helen said, 'I couldn't believe it, you

know, when you and Andrew split up. None of us could. You two always seemed as if you'd been made for each other.'

'I thought so, too, once. . . It just shows how wrong you can be, doesn't it?' There was no disguising the bitter note in Georgina's voice.

'You must both have been very young when you met,' said Helen.

'We were. I was sixteen and Andrew was eighteen.'

'So, how did you meet?'

'He came into the café where I was working during the school holidays.' Georgina gave a rueful smile. Usually she found it too painful to talk of such things but somehow it was different with Helen.

'I was only twenty when we got married. Neither of us had finished training. . .I suppose we were too young, really.'

'I remember your wedding day,' said Helen thoughtfully. 'Like I say, I thought you seemed made for each other. . .'

Georgina shrugged. 'Well, there's no point dwelling on what might been. It's over, and that's that. So, let's get back to this job business. If I was interested—and I am only saying if, mind—when would the job take effect? It might be difficult, with Christmas coming up. . .'

'It wouldn't be until just after Christmas,' replied Helen, then added, 'That's when Janet leaves to go to Canada to live.'

'So, if I decided,' said Georgina slowly, 'what would I have to do about applying? Honestly, Helen, I'm so out of touch.'

'Well,' Helen replied, 'you'd have to go through all the usual channels, of course. Fill in an application form, go for an interview—that sort of thing. But I would be more than happy to give you a reference and that's got

to count for something, even if I do say so myself.' She
gave a short laugh.

'Right. So. . .just supposing, after I'd thought it all
through,' said Georgina slowly, 'I decided to apply—
where would I get an application form?'

'Funny you should say that.' Helen set her own cup
and saucer down, picked up her leather shoulder-bag
from the floor and began to rummage around inside.
'Because I just happen to have brought one with me.'

Much later, after Helen had gone and the two girls
were asleep in bed, Georgina read through the application
form and job description. The thought of returning to
nursing excited her, even if at the same time she felt a
certain apprehension over the time lapse. There were, as
she knew—and as Helen had taken pains to point out—
plenty of refresher courses and study day-releases to
enable her to catch up with modern techniques and procedures.

Where the girls were concerned, she knew she would
have support from her friend, Jeanne, who lived a few
doors away and whose own children she helped to look
after at times, and, indeed, from her own mother who
had cared for Lauren when Georgina had returned to
work after her daughter's birth.

So why this knot of anxiety which had formed in the
pit of her stomach ever since Helen had told her about
the job?

Standing up, she switched off the television, which
she hadn't been watching anyway and which she only
had on for company, and began to prepare for bed. Maybe
if she slept on the problem it would all seem clearer in
the morning. Andrew had always said that if he'd been
troubled by anything. Sleep on it, before making a
decision.

Which was pretty ironic really under the circumstances, thought Georgina as she began to climb the

stairs, when you considered that Andrew was the cause of the anxiety in the first place. Because deep in her heart she knew that if it hadn't been for Andrew, working on the same unit, she would have jumped at Helen's suggestion.

At the top of the stairs she paused and, leaving the dim light burning on the landing, she crept softly into the girls' bedroom.

They were both asleep, Lauren with her long hair spread across the pillow and her sweet face peaceful and Natasha, her dark curls tousled and her bottom in the air as she burrowed into her pillow.

With a smile, Georgina pulled the duvet over her younger daughter then stood quietly for a moment, watching them both. She was about to move away when the light from the landing caught the silver of a photograph frame on the bedside table beside Lauren.

Bending forward, Georgina lifted the frame and stared down at Andrew's handsome face—the dark eyes and brows, the Roman-shaped nose and the untidily casual dark hair. That photograph had been taken in happier times when they had still been together. It was Lauren's favourite of her father and, together with her pony books and rosettes, was among her most treasured possessions.

Was she simply being ridiculous about not wanting to work with Andrew? After all, what harm could it do? They were divorced now—a divorce she had instigated so why should she deny herself the chance not only of a job but also of a return to her career?

Quietly she replaced the photograph, slipped out of the girls' bedroom and into the bathroom. By the time, some little while later, that she went into her own bedroom and closed the door she had almost convinced herself that applying for the job would be the right thing to do.

He had a girlfriend. Another girlfriend. Not Rachel—she'd long gone.

Georgina sat before her dressing-table and stared at her reflection. But was it so strange that he should have another girlfriend? Andrew, after all, was a very attractive man.

She was young, Natasha had said, this girlfriend. Too young, Lauren had said. But Lauren was prejudiced where Andrew was concerned and Georgina doubted whether any woman would meet her elder daughter's high standards.

With a little sigh she picked up her hairbrush and began to draw it through her long brown hair. What was it Andrew had said today? That she looked peaky.

What did peaky actually mean? she wondered.

Tired? Well, that was no wonder, with two healthy children to look after.

Old? Surely not old. He hadn't meant she was looking old, had he?

She turned her head, at the same time lifting her chin. Her neck wasn't lined and the skin around her jawline was as firm as ever. Leaning forward slightly, she peered at her face. There were faint lines around her eyes, but they were laughter lines and, surely, everyone had those.

Her eyes themselves were large and clear—neither brown nor yet quite hazel, a sort of in between colour—but where once they had sparkled with merriment now there was a sadness in their depths which certainly hadn't been there before.

Could that be what peaky meant? That sadness?

Well, if that was the case then Andrew only had himself to blame.

Angrily she dragged the brush through her hair, tangling it and pulling so that the tears sprang to her eyes. How dared he! What right did he have to make such observations? Come to that, what right did he have to still exert influence over any decision she might make?

Abruptly she stood up and untied the belt of her bathrobe. I bet he wouldn't tell his new girlfriend if she looked peaky.

What had Natasha said the girl's name was? Deanne? No, not Deanne. Denise. That was it, Denise White. Natasha had called her trendy. Was she, Georgina, still trendy or had she become hopelessly out of touch? Was she looking peaky because she had become so bogged down by domesticity?

Maybe it really was time she got herself back into the workplace again and became something other than the girls' mother and Andrew Merrick's ex-wife. And it could be something of a shock to Andrew if she suddenly turned up at his place of work. Might even cramp his style a bit.

Georgina gave a grim little smile, took off her bathrobe and slipped into bed, but even before she'd turned out the light she had made her decision and, without needing to sleep on it, knew exactly what she was going to do.

Georgie told the girls what she had decided the following evening after she'd filled in the application form and posted it.

Their response was predictable. Lauren seemed quietly happy that her parents would possibly be spending more time together, while Natasha seemed mainly concerned with who would look after them while her mother was working.

'You'll be at school most of the time,' Georgina said, then went on to reassure her daughter; 'Aunty Jeanne will help out and Granny says she'll come here if necessary or you could go to her.'

This seemed to satisfy Natasha and little more was said until the day of the interview when something of

Georgina's tension seemed to have transmitted itself to the girls.

'Good luck, Mum,' said Lauren seriously.

'You'll be the bestest one there,' said Natasha cheerfully as she scrambled from the car and ran into school.

It was a still, rather damp morning, and as Georgina drove in through the gates of the Shalbrooke General a host of memories surfaced.

This was the hospital where she'd done her training all those years ago, the hospital where she'd gone on to get her first job on Accident and Emergency and the hospital where Andrew had come to work—first as a junior doctor and then as Casualty Officer, and where he was now well on the way to his consultancy.

She sat in the car for a long moment, gazing up at the building of mellow red brick beneath its pink tiled roof. It was also the hospital where both Lauren and later Natasha had been born in the maternity unit.

It had been a long time since she'd last set foot in the place. In fact, she had difficulty remembering exactly when that had been. It had probably been with Andrew to some staff function in the social club, and that would have been a long time ago for she most certainly hadn't been here since her divorce.

But now here she was again. With a sigh she got out of her car, locked it and began to walk toward the front entrance. Here she was, arriving for an interview, every bit as nervous as she'd been all those years ago when she'd applied the first time around.

The glass doors opened automatically. That was different, Georgina thought. In the foyer soft carpet tiles had taken the place of the old black and white shiny ones, but inside a wave of nostalgia swept over her.

There were the familiar smells—that curious combination of antiseptic, cooking, of fresh paint and the scent of flowers. Familiar sounds—of voices, of clatter from the ward sluices and the kitchens, of ringing telephones and buzzers, and porters whistling. And the sights, once so familiar but now almost forgotten—uniformed figures, patients on trolleys *en route* for Theatre, tables outside wards filled with vases of flowers... Nothing appeared to have changed.

Taking a deep breath, Georgina made her way down the endless corridors to the nursing manager's office. Pausing only to smooth down her skirt and adjust the jacket of her suit, she lifted her hand to knock on the closed door.

CHAPTER TWO

THERE was something decidedly forlorn about that period of time between Christmas and New Year, Sister Helen Turner thought as she stood outside her office and gazed around Reception. It was like being in some sort of limbo between one set of festivities and the next.

Not that her own circumstances that Christmas had been particularly festive, with her father the way he was. In a way she was glad to be back at work. At least it gave her something else to think about, and she knew her father was safe and well looked after on the day care unit.

Leaning across the desk, she had just rescued a stray strand of tinsel that was trailing from a fluorescent strip light when the double doors swung open and Elliot Ferguson, A and E's nursing manager, arrived for the morning shift.

'Morning Helen.' He nodded towards her on the way to his office.

'Elliot.' She nodded back, then followed him.

'What excitement do we have this morning?'

'Dare I say that everything seems quiet at the moment?' Helen gave a wry smile as Elliot slipped off his jacket, then opened his briefcase and pulled out a bundle of folders.

'Good,' he said briskly. 'I've got masses of paperwork to do. Couldn't get it done at home—too many relatives in the house.'

'I know what you mean.' Helen pulled a face. 'I'll be glad when everything's back to normal again. Christmas was fine when it was two days, but these days it seems to stretch to two weeks.'

Elliot nodded in weary agreement. 'Who's on today?' he asked.

'Stephanie and Dot,' Helen replied. 'And Andrew. At least I think it was his car I saw in the car park when I came in. . .'

'I say,' Elliot suddenly interrupted her as she would have carried on with the staff list, 'isn't it today that Georgina Merrick starts?'

Helen nodded. 'I was coming to that. Yes, it is today.'

'I hope we don't live to regret that decision,' he said.

'I don't see why we should,' Helen replied calmly. 'I've worked with Georgina before and she's a first-class staff nurse.'

'I'm not doubting her nursing abilities.' Elliot turned as he spoke, filled his coffee-machine with water, then plugged it in and switched on. 'I was merely questioning the ethics of allowing a woman to work in such close proximity to her ex-husband.'

'I'm sure there won't be a problem,' said Helen. 'Andrew and Georgina are on very civilised terms. They have to be because of their children and, besides, they are both highly professional people. I'm sure they wouldn't allow any personal differences to interfere with their work.'

'We shall see,' said Elliot, adding darkly, 'I only hope you're right.' He paused as Helen turned to go. 'How was your dad over Christmas, Helen?'

'Not too good, really,' she replied. 'It confused him even more, having my sister and her husband and family there.'

'Have they gone now?'

'Yes, thank God. Oh, I don't mean to be unkind,' she added quickly, 'but they simply don't understand. They mean well, I know, but they're not there all the time and. . .' She trailed off as there came a tap on the door. 'What is it, Dot?' she asked as a bright-faced young woman in the uniform of a health support worker opened the door.

'There's been a road traffic accident,' said Dot. 'Pedestrian knocked over by a delivery van. Oh, yes, and the new staff nurse, Georgina Merrick, has just arrived. Do you want me to show her round?'

'No, it's all right,' said Helen, following Dot out of the room. 'I'm on my way. I'll do it myself.'

Georgina had been pleased to see Dot Sharman when she'd arrived on the accident and emergency unit that morning. Dot had been brought up in the same village as herself, and although she didn't know her that well it was nice to see a vaguely familiar face.

While Dot went to tell Helen Turner that she had arrived Andrew suddenly appeared, almost, it seemed, from nowhere—as if he had been watching, waiting for her.

'Hello,' he said. His white coat was undone, his stethoscope protruded from his top pocket, his dark hair was untidy and his smile was as devastatingly heart-stopping as ever.

'Hello, Andrew,' Georgina replied, as casually as she could. She had wondered how he would react to the fact that she would be working alongside him at the Shalbrooke.

But when she had received the letter, telling her that her interview had been successful and offering her the job, and the girls—bursting with excitement—had rung their father to tell him the news it hadn't seemed to come as any great surprise—leaving Georgina to assume that he had already been made aware of the situation.

'This is quite like old times, isn't it?' He grinned down

at her and, not giving her a chance to contradict him, he said, 'Are the girls all right?'

'You only saw them the day before last,' she replied evenly, already wishing that the circumstances of this job could have been otherwise and that they would be working in different departments or, ideally, in different premises.

'Yes,' he agreed, 'that's true, I did, and a very good Christmas Day it was as well. Did you have a good day?'

'It was very quiet, with just Mum and me,' Georgina replied tersely. 'But we more than made up for it yesterday.'

'I was rather hoping you would let me take the girls to the pantomime at the weekend,' said Andrew.

'I've already booked seats,' she said crisply.

'Pity. On the other hand, perhaps we should all go together. . .'

'I hardly think that's a good idea—' Georgina began, then broke off as Helen suddenly appeared in Reception, pushing open the double doors.

'Georgina,' she said, 'there you are. Dot said you'd arrived. Good morning, Andrew. . . Glad you're here, too. I understand an RTA is imminent. Now, if you'll excuse us, I'll take Georgina into the office and explain a few things.'

Andrew looked a bit taken aback, disappointed even, as if he had expected to show Georgina the ropes, which really, she thought as she thankfully followed Helen to her office, was ridiculous. After all, in what other circumstances would a casualty officer condescend to show a new member of the nursing staff around the place? Because that was exactly what she was, and while everything at the Shalbrooke seemed vaguely familiar it was at the same time very different from what it had been when Georgina had worked there before.

She spent the first half-hour with Helen, who explained

rotas and shifts to her and then took her to the nurses' staffroom where she changed into her blue and white uniform.

Even that was different, both in design and shade, thought Georgina as she fastened her silver buckle and secured her fob watch. Heaven only knew what other things had changed when it came to nursing techniques. She only hoped she wouldn't show herself up too much in front of the rest of the staff.

When she emerged at last from the staffroom and presented herself in the nurses' station Helen, who must have sensed her apprehension, gave her a reassuring smile and proceeded to introduce her to the rest of the staff. Some she knew, like Elliot, who had interviewed her, and Dot Sharman, of course. She also knew the other sister, Stephanie Miles, by sight as her daughter attended the same school as Lauren and Natasha. But the rest, as Helen named them, became a blur of names and faces, and Georgina found herself wondering if she would ever remember them and be able to distinguish who was who.

Helen assigned her to 'walking wounded', as the non-urgent cases were referred to.

'We'll break you in gently this morning,' she told her. 'You can go with Dot in a minute and she'll show you the drill, but first I'll just show you the treatment rooms.'

'Oh, I know where those are,' said Georgina quickly, not wanting to waste Helen's time on trivialities.

'I think you may find they've changed slightly from what you remember.' Helen chuckled as she led the way into the larger of two emergency treatment rooms.

'That's probably the understatement of the decade.' In dismay, Georgina gazed around her at the alarming array of modern equipment, monitors and hydraulic beds. 'I don't know about a refresher course,' she said. 'Looking at this lot, I would say I need to retrain.'

'You're not to worry about it,' said Helen firmly. 'At

the end of the day nursing is mainly about people, and they don't change. The ones we see in here are just as shocked, bewildered and frightened as they ever were. If I remember rightly, you were first class at dealing with that sort of thing, and you will soon get the hang of this lot.' She waved her hand towards the equipment. 'That is something that can be taught—the right approach is something else entirely.'

'Well, it's good of you to say so,' Georgina muttered as she followed Helen into the smaller of the treatment rooms. 'I only hope I live up to your expectations.'

The large treatment room had been empty. 'It's usually quiet in this aftermath of Christmas,' Helen had explained, but there were two patients in the smaller room. One was a very elderly man who appeared to be asleep while the other, a little girl, was sobbing bitterly. Andrew was crouched beside her bed, talking quietly to her and smoothing her long blonde hair back from her damp little face. He looked up as Georgina and Helen approached.

'This is Jessica,' he said. 'She's had a fall from her new bicycle. We're going to take some photographs of your leg, aren't we, Jessica?'

Jessica hiccuped. 'Mum—Mummy will be cross,' she said. 'My bike is all broken.'

'Is her mother here?' Helen glanced at a nurse who was attending to the other patient.

'She's on her way, apparently.' The nurse, a pretty girl whose name escaped Georgina, turned from the bed. 'A neighbour brought Jessica in.' The nurse lowered her voice so that the little girl wouldn't hear. 'Honestly, I don't know what some parents are thinking about. Fancy letting her out on her own like that on a new bike.'

'They probably didn't know,' remarked Andrew cryptically. 'Children of that age have the knack of disappearing,' he added, his gaze almost magnetically drawn to Georgina's. 'Remember that time Natasha wandered off on the beach? We only took our eyes off her for a moment, didn't we?'

Georgina found herself nodding in agreement.

'Georgina was drying Lauren, who'd just come out of the water,' Andrew went on, 'and I was searching for the suncream in the beach-bag. When I looked up Natasha was gone. Absolute panic stations.'

As he rolled his eyes heavenwards just for one moment Georgina relived that terrible time when they had gradually become convinced that Natasha had either wandered into the sea and been drowned or had been lured away by some perverted character with evil intent.

'So, what happened?' asked the nurse curiously.

'After a frantic search, and when everyone was on the point of calling the police, the coastguard and every other emergency service, we found her,' said Andrew.

'Where was she?' The nurse turned to Georgina.

'About twenty yards away, building a sandcastle with a group of children,' Georgina answered. 'She couldn't understand what all the fuss was about.'

'I can see I've got a lot to learn where children are concerned,' the nurse laughed.

Georgina's gaze met Andrew's amused one again, then hastily she looked away towards the other patient. 'Is that the RTA patient who came in earlier?' she asked quickly. It was far too soon to be sharing memories or experiencing moments of enforced intimacy with Andrew—in fact, that was the one thing she had been hoping to avoid at all costs. It was just unfortunate that in those first few moments they should have been drawn together on a case involving a child, a little girl who, with her long fair hair, bore a striking resemblance to Lauren, or rather how Lauren had been a few years ago—in happier times.

'Yes.' Andrew, too, seemed to have recovered and,

turning to the elderly man on the second bed, nodded. 'Mr Hamley was on his way to collect his morning paper when he was knocked over by the van which was delivering the papers to the newsagent. He's waiting to go to Theatre with suspected internal injuries.' He turned to Helen. 'Any news on an anaesthetist yet, Sister?'

Helen nodded. 'Yes, Richard Fleetwood is on call. He's on his way in.' She paused and glanced at Georgina. 'Now that you've had a look in here perhaps you'd like to join Dot.'

Carefully avoiding Andrew's eye, Georgina followed Helen from the room. 'Is that Richard Fleetwood the GP you were talking about?' she asked as they walked back to Reception.

'Yes,' Helen nodded. 'He's a part-time consultant anaesthetist. Didn't you know?'

'No, I didn't.' Georgina shook her head.

'Are you registered with him?' asked Helen.

'No, the girls and I are with his partner, Paul Wooldridge. Apparently, Paul's just started a year's sabbatical in Australia so we could well be seeing Dr Fleetwood in the future.'

'I understand they have a locum starting this week,' said Helen.

'I should think they'll need it,' replied Georgina. 'They always seem so busy whenever I go to the surgery.'

'You mean like this?' Helen grinned as they stepped back into Reception.

As they'd approached Georgina had been aware of a growing hubbub, but she wasn't quite prepared for the crowd of patients that met her gaze.

'Wherever did this lot come from?' she gasped. 'This was empty only a moment ago. I thought you said it would be quiet this morning.'

Helen laughed. 'They obviously heard me and have done this just to prove me wrong. It's all right, Dot,' she called as they caught a glimpse of Dot's frantic expression as she pulled back a curtain round one of the cubicles. 'We're with you, aren't we, Georgie?'

'Yes,' agreed Georgina faintly, 'I suppose we are.'

She very quickly became absorbed into the busy routine and in no time at all began to feel as if she'd never been away from nursing. As Helen had pointed out, people don't change and the patients and their ailments were little different from those that Georgina recalled from her earlier nursing days—a woman with burns to her hands and arms from oil from a hot chip-pan, a toddler with a bead up his nose, a young man who had been a passenger in a car involved in a collision and who had suffered whiplash injuries. Each was assessed and dealt with—the burns dressed, the bead removed and the young man fitted with a supporting neck brace.

Dot was pleasant and easygoing to work with, and when a doctor was required to see a patient it was A and E's junior doctor, Susan Joliffe, who came into the cubicles—and not Andrew—so there were no more awkward moments.

When it was time for Georgina's coffee-break she took herself off to a corner of the staffroom where, after a few moments, she was joined by the young nurse who had been in the treatment room.

'Phew!' The girl sat down in an easy chair and kicked off her shoes. 'I'd expected it to be quiet today—just shows how wrong you can be.'

'Coffee?' Georgina stood and picked up the coffee-jug.

'Please.' The girl nodded and watched as Georgina filled a mug then as she handed it to her, curling her hands around it. 'Thanks,' she said, taking a sip.

She really was a very pretty girl, Georgina thought as she watched her for a moment, before sitting down again. She only looked about twenty-one or -two and had short

blonde hair cut into a wispy urchin-cut that framed her
tiny face and delicate features.

'Ah, that's better,' the girl sighed and leaned her head
against the back of her chair. 'I'm shattered,' she said
after a moment, 'although it's my own fault—too many
late nights, I expect.'

'Sounds as if you've had a good Christmas,' said
Georgina, trying to remember what it had been like when
she had been young and without family ties at the festive
season.

'You could say that. I spent most of it with my boyfriend,' the girl grinned. 'That's probably why I'm tired.
What about you—what did you do?'

'Oh, I had a very quiet Christmas Day,' said Georgina.
'Boxing Day was a little more lively with my daughters
and other family members. . .' She trailed off as the door
opened and Andrew strolled into the room.

'Hi,' he said, 'surviving your first morning?'

'Just about.' She drained her cup and stood up. 'I'd
better be getting back.'

'Don't go on my account,' he said easily.

'I was going, anyway,' she replied. 'We were just
chatting about Christmas, weren't we. . .?' She glanced
at the girl. 'I'm so sorry, I didn't catch your name.'

'That's OK,' said the girl pleasantly. 'It's Denny.'

'Denny. . .?' Georgina paused, she wasn't sure why,
and the girl misinterpreted her hesitancy.

'Yes, short for Denise. . .that's my name, really, but
everyone calls me Denny.'

She didn't say her surname but she didn't have to
because quite suddenly, without any doubt, Georgina
knew who she was.

Without speaking—without even acknowledging what
the girl had said—Georgina looked at Andrew, but he
had his back to them and was pouring his own coffee.
What was it Natasha had said that day when she'd

scrambled into the car? 'Daddy's got a girlfriend.' That
was it, plain and simple. 'Daddy's got a girlfriend.'

Turning abruptly, and without so much as another
glance at the other two occupants, Georgina left the
staffroom.

She should have known, she told herself angrily as
she hurried down the corridor back to Reception. She'd
already noticed how pretty the girl was. . .and how
young. Natasha had said she was young, but how could
she have known. . .? It hadn't even registered in her mind
when Helen had introduced the girl, along with all the
others. . . And, besides, she'd probably referred to her as
Denny, if that was what everyone called the girl, whereas
Natasha had called her Denise.

Natasha would have called her that if that was what
Andrew called her, and that, Georgina knew, was exactly
what Andrew would have done. He hated abbreviations
of people's names—he always used their full names. He
always called her Georgina where others often called her
Georgie, and now here he was calling Denny Denise.

She should have known.

But how could she have known? She'd had no other
details about this girl except that she was young, and
that Lauren thought she was too young for her father.
But she should have guessed that she probably worked
at the hospital with Andrew.

The other one had worked at the hospital. . . Rachel.
She'd been a radiologist. . . She, too, had worked alongside Andrew. . . She mustn't start thinking about her now,
Georgina thought desperately, because she would only
become bitter, angry and upset. She must push the painful
memories right to the back of her mind where they
belonged.

But she still wished she'd known about this one—
about Denise, or Denny, or whatever she called herself.
And if she had known, she asked herself as she angrily

pushed open the double doors to Reception and strode
through, would it have made any difference? Would she
still have applied for this job?

Of course she would, she told herself firmly. She
simply couldn't let that sort of thing dictate her future.
Her relationship with Andrew was firmly in the past
where it belonged. What he did now or with whom was
no business of hers, any more than what she did was
anything to do with him.

'How did you get on?'

'Did you see Daddy?'

The girls pounced on her the minute she returned.

'Hey, one at a time.' Georgina laughed and hugged
them both. 'I got on very well, better than I thought I
would. . .'

'But did you see Daddy?' This was from Natasha, a
wide-eyed, excited Natasha.

'Of course she saw Dad,' said Lauren scathingly. 'He
works there, too, silly.'

'I'm not silly.' Natasha pouted. 'I'm not silly, am
I, Mummy?'

'No, darling, you're not silly,' said Georgina, frowning
slightly at her elder daughter and shaking her head.
Lauren bothered her sometimes. She seemed to have
grown up very quickly since the divorce and had taken
on attitudes and responsibilities far beyond her years.
'And, yes, I did see Daddy.'

'Did you work with him?' Natasha obviously needed
more details. 'Bandaging and things?'

'Not exactly, not today. Daddy was working mainly
in the treatment rooms where they deal with all the
big accidents—you know, the people who arrive by
ambulance.'

'So where were you?' Lauren had been about to pour
herself a glass of orange juice from a carton she'd taken

from the fridge but she paused, carton poised, and stared at Georgina.

'I was attending to those patients whose injuries were not quite so serious. People who had made their own way to the hospital.'

'What sort of injuries?' demanded Natasha, dumping the shocking-pink nylon bag she'd taken to Jeanne's house in one corner of the kitchen and struggling up onto one of the high stools at the breakfast bar.

'Burns, minor bumps and grazes, small cuts that needed stitching—that sort of thing,' explained Georgina.

'Sounds boring,' said Natasha. 'What was Daddy doing?'

'Dealing with road accidents, and big emergencies like heart attacks. . .'

'That sounds much more exciting,' Natasha breathed.

Georgina laughed. 'Sounds as if you're still interested in becoming a nurse.'

'I might be.' Natasha sighed and took an apple from a bowl on the bar, biting noisily into it. 'Or I thought I might work in a fish shop.'

'A fish shop?' Georgina stared incredulously at her younger daughter. 'Whatever brought that on?'

'I love watching Mr Buxton when we go to his shop,' sighed Natasha ecstatically. 'When he slaps the fish onto that slab it makes such a lovely noise.'

'You'd pong dreadfully.' Lauren wrinkled her nose distastefully.

Georgina laughed again and then, as she began taking vegetables from the rack to prepare for their evening meal, she said, 'No need to ask if you've changed your mind about what you want to do.'

'I shall never change my mind,' said Lauren.

'You need your own horse if you're going to be a

showjumper,' said Natasha. 'I heard Mrs Mitchell up at the stables say that.'

'I don't care,' said Lauren hotly.

'I was only saying. . .' Natasha shrugged. 'And, anyway, you'd pong as well from the horses. . .'

'All right, girls,' Georgina stepped in smartly, 'that's enough. We all know it would be better if Lauren had her own pony but we can't afford one so that's all there is to it.'

That put paid to the matter, for the time being at least, although Georgina knew it would remain an issue while Lauren pursued this particular ambition. The girls continued to question her about her day, mainly over her dealings with Andrew, but it was much later when Natasha was in the bath and she and Lauren were briefly alone that Georgina posed the question which had been niggling all afternoon.

'Lauren,' she said as casually as she could, 'did you know that that girl, Denise, works at the hospital with Daddy?'

Lauren frowned. 'Does she? I don't think they said that.'

'Have you seen her again when you've been to your father's?'

'She came skating with us again.'

'I see.' Georgina paused. 'What about Christmas Day? Was she there then?'

Lauren shook her head. 'No, only Daddy, Grandma and Grandpa and us.'

'Ah. . .'

'But—'

'Yes?' she said quickly. 'What?'

'We came home after tea, didn't we?'

'Yes. . .'

'I think something was happening in the evening. . .'

'Weren't Grandma and Grandpa going to their friend's house in Cowes?'

'Yes, but I don't think Dad was going with them. I heard him say, "Do I have to go?" Then Grandma laughed and said, "No," and that she was sure he had far better things to do than sit and talk about the old days with a group of old. . .codgers. I think that's what she said. . .'

'Probably,' said Georgina dryly. 'Your father always could wind your grandma round his little finger. . . So, did he say what the something better was?'

'No.' Lauren shook her head, and a moment later she added, 'I still think she's too young for him. I told him so as well.'

'Did you?' Georgina stared at her daughter in awe. 'What did he say?'

'He laughed and called me a little minx.'

'What's a minx?' asked Natasha, suddenly appearing in the bedroom doorway, with a towel wrapped turban-style around her head.

'I told you to wait,' said Georgina sharply. 'That I would wash your hair for you.'

'Oh, I haven't washed it,' said Natasha airily.

'So why have you got that towel round your head?' demanded Lauren.

'Because I like it,' said Natasha. 'It makes me feel like an Arab princess—and I do know what a minx is. I've just remembered—it's a little furry animal they use to make fur coats.'

'That's a mink!' said Lauren, rolling her eyes. 'I said she was silly,' she added to Georgina.

The matter ended there as Georgina was caught up in the girls' needs but later that night her mind drifted back to her new job, to Andrew and to his girlfriend. It was inevitable, really, that he should find someone else, she thought as she tidied up the kitchen. She supposed she should do the same. There had been no one for her since Andrew.

All the men she knew were either married or divorced, and the few divorced ones she'd spoken to seemed to be weighed down with so many problems, both emotional and practical, that Georgina had been put off even before the point where anyone had actually got as far as asking her out.

And if she did get that far and go out with someone again she wasn't sure how she would behave. Dating was something she associated with teenagers, and she was pretty certain she'd forgotten how to flirt—that was, if she'd ever known in the first place. Andrew had been the only man in her life—the only one she'd ever loved, the only one she'd ever wanted—and certainly the only one she'd ever been to bed with.

And wasn't that taken for granted these days, more often than not after the first date as well, if popular magazines and some television programmes were anything to go by? That was something Georgina would never understand in a million years—how anyone could be that intimate with someone they had only met a few hours before. Probably she was hopelessly old-fashioned, but she couldn't help it and neither did she care. There had been a time when she had thought Andrew felt the same way. But that had been before...before he had betrayed her and broken her heart...

The shrill, persistent ringing of the telephone in the hall broke into her thoughts and, throwing down her teacloth, she hurried to answer it before it woke the girls.

CHAPTER THREE

'IT WAS Andrew. Because Georgina had been thinking of him, all the old anger was close to the surface and her response was sharper than it might have been.

'Oh,' she said, 'it's you.'

'You sound disappointed,' he replied. 'Who were you expecting?'

'No one, really. . .'

'You answered pretty smartly.' She could hear the amusement in his voice and could picture him standing there—could even see the half-smile on his face.

'I didn't want the phone to wake the girls.'

'How are they?'

'That's the second time today you've asked that question, Andrew.'

'Is it? Do you have a problem with that?' She could still hear the faint amusement in his voice.

'No, no, of course not. It just seems a little unusual, that's all.'

'You make it sound as if I don't care about my girls. And I do. Very much '

'I know you do.' She tried to keep the impatience from her voice. 'But I'm sure you didn't ring at this time of night just to tell me that.'

'You're quite right, I didn't. In fact, I rang because this time it was you I was concerned about.'

'Me?' He couldn't have failed to hear the surprise in her voice.

'Again, is that so unusual?' he said, then he gave a short laugh. 'No, don't bother to answer that. . . I merely wondered how you felt after your first day back at work.'

'Oh, oh, I see.' She felt a little foolish. 'Well, my head was spinning when I got home...with everything I'd seen and heard...but, on the whole, I suppose it wasn't too bad.'

'You've been out of nursing for some time—I guess a lot of things are different.'

'Yes, they are,' she agreed, 'and it's going to take a long time to really get back into the swing of things. Helen is going to arrange a refresher course for me and some study days.'

'Good for Helen,' said Andrew, and added, 'She's great, isn't she?'

'Yes, she is,' Georgina agreed, then fell silent. She had the feeling that he wanted to say more.

'Did anyone upset you today?' he asked after a moment.

'Upset me?' she said quickly. 'Why should you think that?'

'I don't know.' He hesitated. 'I'm not sure, that's why I'm asking. It was when I came into the staffroom and you were talking to Denise. Denise White. You know?'

'Yes, Andrew, I know who you mean.'

'Well, you beat such a hasty retreat,' he went on, 'that I found myself wondering if everything was all right.'

'Everything was fine,' Georgina heard herself say. The last thing she wanted was for Andrew to even suspect that she had been thrown by the fact that she was not only to be working alongside him but his girlfriend as well. 'Why shouldn't it be?' she added almost flippantly when he remained silent.

'No reason,' he said, 'no reason at all. I just wondered, that's all. I wouldn't want there to be any embarrassment for you on the unit.'

'I can't see that there should be.' She spoke lightly but found herself gripping the reciver more tightly and sinking down until she was sitting on the edge of the bottom stair.

'Well, I'm glad we agree on that,' he began, but stopped abruptly as she interrupted him.

'While we're on the subject, Andrew,' she said, taking a deep breath, 'there was just one thing. . .'

'Yes,' he said quickly, 'and what's that?'

'I think,' she said, 'that while we are at work we should refrain from discussing any domestic matters.'

'You mean, anything to do with the girls?'

'Partly. . . Well.' It was her turn to hesitate. 'Yes, I suppose that is what I do mean,' she added at last.

'Why?'

'Why what?'

'Why don't you think we should mention the girls?'

'I just don't think it would be a very professional thing to do, that's all.'

'Other members of staff talk about their children.' A stubborn note had crept into his voice now, a note Georgina recognised only too well. 'I don't see why we shouldn't.'

'It's a bit different for other members of staff,' she said tersely. 'They don't have their partners. . .ex-partners,' she hastily corrected herself, 'on the premises, do they?'

'And you think that makes a difference?'

'Yes, Andrew, I do. I'm sorry but that's the way I feel about it.'

'OK,' he said. 'Fine. I'll endeavour to control my natural impulses in future. It won't be easy because I'm used to talking about the girls, but. . .' he gave a sigh which even to Georgina on the other end of the line sounded exaggerated '. . .I'll do my best.'

'Please don't make this any more difficult than it already is,' she said.

'I hadn't thought it was difficult,' he replied. 'Not until a few minutes ago, that is.'

'Are you telling me you didn't have any qualms about me coming to work on the unit?'

'Why should I have? After all, we have worked together before.'

'That was a very long time ago, Andrew.' She could hear the note of protest in her own voice. 'A lot has happened since then.'

'Yes,' he said softly, 'it certainly has.'

Suddenly she recognised the change in his tone. It was one she had heard so many times before, and she felt a wave of panic sweep over her. 'I really must be going, Andrew,' she said. 'It's getting late and I have an early start. Besides, I dare say you're wanting to get to bed.'

'I am in bed,' he said.

'Oh, are you?' The mental image she'd had of him standing by the phone was gone, replaced by one of him lying alone in bed with the phone tucked under his chin. At least she assumed he was alone. Even as the possibility hit her that Denise White might be with him—lying alongside him and listening to the conversation he had just had with her—she panicked afresh. 'I must go, Andrew. . . Goodbye.'

'Goodnight, Georgina—'

But that was all she heard because by then she had replaced the receiver. For a moment she continued to sit on the stairs, staring at the phone and wondering afresh exactly why he had phoned and if he had indeed been alone or had had company.

'Mum?'

She looked sharply over her shoulder. Lauren was standing at the top of the stairs in her white nightshirt with the frog motif on the front.

'Who was that on the phone?' Sleepily she rubbed her eyes.

'It was Dad,' Georgina said, scrambling to her feet.
'What did he want?'
'Only to see how I got on at work today, that's all.'
'But he was there, wasn't he?'
'Yes, but we weren't actually working together,' she
said as she reached the top of the stairs. 'Come on, you
must get back to bed or you won't be up for school in
the morning. I'm sorry the phone woke you.'
'It wasn't the phone,' mumbled Lauren. 'I heard you
talking.' She allowed Georgina to propel her gently back
into the bedroom where Natasha was sound asleep in her
own bed. 'You weren't arguing, were you?' she whispered urgently as Georgina helped her into bed.
'No,' Georgina whispered back, 'we weren't arguing.'
'That's good.' Lauren sighed as Georgina leaned over
to kiss her and said, 'I still miss Dad, you know.'
'I know you do, Lauren,' she replied gently, smiling
down at her daughter in the half-light and smoothing her
hair back from her forehead. 'Now you go back to sleep.
God bless.'
She had reached the door when Lauren spoke again
in the same loud whisper.
'Mum?'
'Yes, darling?' Georgina paused with one hand on
the door.
'That was nice of Dad to phone, wasn't it?'
'Yes, darling, it was.' Georgina smiled again and
stepped out of the room onto the landing, pulling the
door to behind her.

The following day Georgina drove to the hospital, having
already decided that any future contact with Andrew
while they were both in uniform was to be of a strictly
professional nature. Likewise, she had also decided that
the same applied to Denise White. She would be pleasant

to them both but would do nothing to encourage confidences of a personal nature.

The recent spell of damp, foggy weather had given way to frost, and the morning was crisp and dry with an icy blue sky. Rooks cawed from the tops of the tall trees that lined the road, and as she left the mudflats of Newtown Creek and took the Porchfield road the frost-covered fields and hedgerows on either side sparkled in the pale wintry sunshine.

Shalbrooke had once been a hamlet which had grown into a village and which now—with its new status as home to the Island's second hospital, and together with a complex of new houses and a shopping mall—threatened to become a small town. It lay tucked beneath the ridge of chalk downs that formed the Island's backbone, facing the open countryside and villages to the north of the Island. Beyond, brief glimpses of the Solent and its busy shipping lanes could be seen.

The hospital itself was on a large site, partly wooded with beeches, oaks and conifers and with a huge ornamental lake in the centre, home to carp and other more exotic species of fish. To the left of the hospital beside the shops and backed by the playing fields of the local comprehensive school stood the Fleetwood Medical Centre. As Georgina drove into the hospital car park another car drew up alongside her and she realised that the driver was Richard Fleetwood.

'Good morning,' he said as he got out of his car. 'It's Mrs Merrick, isn't it?'

'Yes, good morning, Doctor.' Georgina smiled as she got out of her car and locked it. They walked together to the main entrance and Georgina remembered that Helen had said that Richard Fleetwood was a part-time anaesthetist at the hospital.

'Not a patient, I hope?' he said as he held the door open for her.

'No,' she shook her head, 'far from it. I work here now.'

'Really?' He sounded surprised but pleased. 'How's it working out?'

'I'm not sure yet,' Georgina laughed. 'Maybe you'd better ask me that question again in a few weeks' time. I only started yesterday.'

They were both laughing as they approached A and E Reception. Helen was behind the desk and she looked up.

'Hello,' she said easily. 'Good, two of you together—that means I can kill two birds with one stone.'

'That sounds ominous.' Richard Fleetwood pulled a face. 'What is it this time—a raffle, a charity walk?'

'No,' said Helen sweetly, 'nothing like that. It's the New Year's Eve staff party.'

'Oh, God!' groaned Richard. 'Am I really expected to go to that?'

'Of course,' Helen replied. 'You'd have been most offended if you hadn't been asked. You know you would. And while we're on the subject your staff are included in that invitation as well.'

Muttering to himself, Richard went off in the direction of Theatre but not before he had winked at Georgina.

'You'll be coming, Georgie, won't you?' said Helen, her pen poised over the clipboard she was carrying.

'Oh, I don't know about that, Helen,' Georgina replied. 'I really don't.'

'But you must. It's a great party—it always is.'

'I have the girls to consider,' said Georgina.

'Wouldn't your mum babysit for you?'

'She may do. . .'

'Normally I'd say ask Andrew, but you can hardly do that on this occasion, can you?' Helen laughed. 'Seeing he'll be there.'

I bet he will, thought Georgina gloomily as she left Helen and made her way to the staffroom to change, along with his girlfriend, the rest of the staff and old Uncle Tom Cobbley and all.

That morning, to her consternation, Georgina found herself allocated to the treatment rooms. She had hoped that Helen would keep her on walking wounded, at least until she'd done some refresher work, but it wasn't Helen who sent her there but Elliot. He must, however, have seen her doubtful expression.

'You need to familiarise yourself with the workings of the whole unit,' he said, 'but, don't worry, there are plenty of others around this morning to give you a hand. And, while we're on the subject, we've had details of the first of your refresher lectures. I believe they start some time early in the New Year.'

'That's a relief,' said Georgina. 'I must admit most things are instinct or common sense but the new technology frightens me to death.'

The treatment room was empty when she arrived and she took the opportunity to examine some of the equipment, but her exploration exercise proved short-lived for within five minutes an ambulance had arrived and the paramedics, Dave Morey and Pete Steel, were carrying in the first of the morning's casualties.

Helen was accompanying them and asking questions as the patient was transferred from their trolley to an examination bed. At first glance Georgina could see that the patient was male and middle-aged, his complexion ashen beneath what was obviously usually a weather-beaten, rugged exterior.

'Do we know his name?' asked Helen, motioning to Georgina to assist with the transfer.

Dave Morey nodded. 'Yes, it's Jack—Jack Oakley. Isn't that right, Jack?' he addressed the patient, who appeared only semi-conscious.

Georgina, who knew the patient slightly by sight, noticed that he was already on a saline drip which the paramedics had set up. She was about to ask what had happened to him when Andrew suddenly appeared in the treatment room.

'Oh, good,' said Helen, 'here's Dr Merrick now.'

'What do we have?' asked Andrew, looking down at the patient.

'Farm accident.' It was Dave Morey who replied. 'Mr Oakley here lives up at Hailes Farm. According to his wife and one of the farm hands, he'd gone out ploughing and had some sort of accident with the tractor. We don't know for sure yet but it looks as if the tractor went right over his legs.'

'Right, Sister.' Andrew glanced at Helen. 'Can we take a look, please?'

To Georgina, who knew him so well, Andrew looked tired, but, then, he probably would be if. . . She swallowed. She mustn't think of that now. Not now when a man's life hung in the balance and everyone's skills were needed. Helen had removed the cellular blankets covering the man and returned them to the paramedics. He was wearing dark blue denims and a padded, red checked shirt over a thick jersey. His grey hair was ruffled and there was dark stubble on his jaw as if he hadn't shaved that morning.

'He's all yours, then,' said Pete Steel, folding the stretcher.

'We'll leave you to it.' Dave grinned at Georgina and narrowed his eyes. 'You're new here, aren't you?' When she nodded in reply he winked, a gesture that wasn't missed by Andrew who raised his eyebrows. 'See you, Jack.' Dave leaned over and spoke to the patient who had opened his eyes and was moaning softly. 'All the best, mate—you're in good hands now—they've got the A team on this morning, by the looks of it.' He grinned and followed Pete out of the treatment room.

'Let's get these clothes cut off,' said Helen, handing Georgina a pair of scissors.

Between them they cut through the tough, blood-soaked denim of Jack Oakley's jeans, gradually revealing as they did so the extent of the man's appalling injuries. Both legs appeared to have been crushed by the weight of the tractor and one was mangled below the knee as if it had been caught in some way by the ploughing machinery.

'We want cross-matching, bloods and X-rays,' said Andrew as he carried out a thorough examination. 'It looks as if blood loss has been severe. Both left and right tibias and fibulas look crushed and the left femur is exposed. Oxygen, please, Nurse,' he said to Georgina, 'and Omnipon for the pain, Sister.'

As Jack Oakley opened his eyes fully Andrew leaned over him. 'Hello,' he said.

'Where am I?' came the inevitable question.

'In hospital, old man,' replied Andrew cheerfully. 'Seems you had a disagreement with your tractor—do you remember?'

'I don't know,' Jack replied. 'She were playin' up. I remembers that. I got off to look, one of the bolts were loose...then...it... Oh, God! Yes, it sheered sideways. I couldn't hold it... Then it rolled on top of me... It seemed like hours... Then...the missus she came with young Ralph and found me...'

'Your wife's outside, Jack,' said Helen as she changed the saline drip.

'She's here?' Jack Oakley, lifting the oxygen mask from his face, sounded surprised.

'Yes.' Helen nodded. 'She's waiting to see you. We'll let her come in when Doctor's finished.'

'Better not let young Ralph in.' Jack suddenly gave a weak chuckle.

'Why's that, Jack?' asked Georgina as she finally

removed the last of the blood-soaked material sticking to the jagged wounds.

'Can't stand the sight of blood,' said Jack. 'Keel over, he would.'

After Jack Oakley's injuries had been assessed, he'd been given painkilling injections and his wife, Heather, had been in to see him. The A and E porters, accompanied by Georgina, took him to the X-ray unit.

By this time Jack had become very subdued and after the X-rays had been completed and he and Georgina were waiting for the porters again he looked up at Georgina and said, 'Reckon that's me finished, then.'

'Well, that's certainly all the X-rays for the moment, Jack,' she replied, 'but they may wish to do more later—'

'No,' he interrupted her with a sigh so deep it could almost have been a sob. 'I didn't mean that. . .I meant I were finished with farming. . .now. . .after this lot. . .'

'Oh, I don't know about that, Jack.' For one moment Georgina didn't know what to say as the sheer hopelessness in the man's attitude suddenly got to her.

'Had a lifetime on the farm, I have. . . Took over from my old dad, and him from his father before him. Built that farm up, we have, between us. . . And now, one silly slip and that's the end of it all. . .'

'You don't know that, Jack,' said Georgina firmly. 'They can do wonders these days, you know. . .'

'With legs in this state?' Jack threw her such a sceptical look that she was forced, on the pretext of looking for the porter, to look away.

Jack was transported back to the treatment room on A and E and when the X-ray plates were available they were carefully examined by Andrew and the rest of the team in the nurses' station.

'The injuries are just as I'd thought,' said Andrew, peering up at the plates, 'although I must say there is more damage to the left femur than I'd realised.'

'There's a lot of splintering to the right tibia,' said Elliot as, watched by Helen, Dot and Georgina, he looked over Andrew's shoulder.

'We need the orthopaedic reg down here.' Andrew glanced round.

'I've already phoned through,' said Helen, 'warning them we'll want a bed and that Mr Oakley will need to go to Theatre. Apparently Neil Baltimore himself is on today. He's coming down in a few minutes.' She smiled at Georgina. 'You can go and tell Jack Oakley that he's got one of the best orthopaedic surgeons in the country. Maybe that will cheer him up a bit.'

'I think it'll take more than that at the moment,' said Andrew. 'The poor chap thinks it's the end of the world. . .or, at least, the end of his world. But tell him, anyway, Georgina. It just might help.' He, too, turned and smiled at her and Georgina had to stifle the little leap of her heart as her eyes met his.

Would that ever stop? she asked herself as she hurried back to the treatment room. Surely it should have done by now.

She found Heather Oakley sitting by her husband's side, gently chafing one of his large, work-roughened hands between hers. She glanced up at Georgina as she approached. She was tall and large-boned, her grey hair sensibly cut and her complexion ruddy from a lifetime in the open air.

'Mrs Oakley.' Georgina looked down at Jack who had his eyes closed. 'I've just come to tell you that the surgeon is on his way to see your husband. According to my colleagues, he's apparently one of the best in the country so I thought you might like to know that Jack's going to be in good hands.'

'Thank you, Nurse. That's good of you.' Heather Oakley gave a weary smile, and as Georgina straightened the covers and checked on Jack's drip she added softly, 'Strange how things happen, isn't it?'

'What do you mean?' Georgina had been about to move away but she paused.

'I've been on at Jack for several years now to slow down, to think about selling the farm so that we can enjoy some retirement together, but would he listen? Stubborn as a mule he is, like most men.' Shaking her head, she stared down at her husband.

'You married, Nurse?' she said after a moment, then added, 'Oh, yes, I see you are.' She glanced at Georgina's left hand, her gaze falling on the plain gold wedding band that she still wore. 'No doubt you'll know what I mean. Think they know best, then it takes something like this to show them they don't. Your husband stubborn, is he?'

Out of the corner of her eye Georgina was aware that Andrew had come into the treatment room together with Richard Fleetwood, the duty anaesthetist for that day, and a tall distinguished-looking man in a grey suit who she guessed must be Neil Baltimore, the consultant ortho-paedic surgeon. Suddenly she knew that Andrew had heard Heather Oakley's question and was also waiting to see what her reply would be.

'Er. . . Like you say, Mrs Oakley,' she murmured, 'it does seem to be a common trait.'

She saw Andrew's lips twitch and the amusement in his dark eyes as she moved to the back of the little group. Jack Oakley opened his eyes and Mr Baltimore drew a chair forward in order to sit and talk to his patient.

Throughout the consultation she was acutely aware of Andrew by her side and it took a few minutes for her to realise that she hadn't corrected Heather Oakley when she had alluded to her having a husband. She should have done. She should automatically have said that she was divorced. It wouldn't have made any difference to Heather Oakley, but somehow it seemed to imply something about Georgina's state of mind, insomuch that after two years, on the spur of the moment when challenged, she still thought of herself as being married instead of divorced.

Maybe it had been a mistake after all to be working in such close proximity to Andrew. She knew him too well, knew what his reactions would be to almost any situation and knew also that the reverse was true—that he could anticipate almost her every move. By the same token, it was probably impossible to dismantle in two or three years something that had taken sixteen or so years to build.

Briefly, as Andrew began talking to Richard Fleetwood, Georgina allowed her thoughts to wander back down the years, a dangerous pursuit, she knew, and one which she very rarely allowed herself to do. She had loved him on sight, if such a thing was possible.

Her friend at the time, a girl called Cathy Jones—a fellow waitress at the café—had told her there was no such thing as love at first sight, that you couldn't love someone in such a short space of time, only fancy them, and that what Georgina felt was undoubtedly lust. But Georgina didn't care what her friend said. She knew she'd loved Andrew from the moment he'd strolled into the café, sat at a corner table and ordered a coffee from her.

'Anything to eat, sir?' she'd said, aware that the look in his eyes had caused her cheeks to turn red.

'No, just a coffee, thanks.'

She didn't know how she hadn't spilt the coffee or at least slopped it in the saucer as she'd set it down in front of him, and when he'd asked her what time she finished work she couldn't remember having answered him. But she must have done because he'd been waiting outside for her when she'd finished.

'What would you like to do?' he said.

'I have to catch my bus at eight o'clock,' she replied, her heart thumping so hard she feared she was about to suffocate. 'But we could walk for a while,' she added hastily, afraid he might go.

And walk they had, the full length of the Esplanade to the pier, with Georgina desperately hoping she would be seen by someone from school. Anyone would do because the word would get round that Georgina Bailey had been seen with this fabulous-looking boy.

'Can I buy you an ice cream?' he asked when they reached the pier. They sat on the railings, licking strawberry-flavoured cornets, and Georgina learned he lived in Portsmouth but that he was spending part of his holiday with his aunt who ran a seaside guest-house. In the last of the evening sunshine he walked her to the bus stop and saw her safely aboard the bus.

After that he met her every day from work while she counted the hours until she would see him again.

On the third evening they paddled together in the sea through the shallow water and he had teased her about something—she couldn't remember what. She splashed him in retaliation and he chased her, finally catching her and trapping her against one of the lichen-covered stone pillars supporting the pier. Gasping, she turned to face him and he put his hands either side of her on the pillar, imprisoning her.

Then the laughing stopped and his lips gently, very gently at first, covered hers. If for Georgina there had been any slight doubt about love at first sight, it was in that moment finally banished because she knew then that she really did love him.

He explained to her that they wouldn't be able to see much of each other. He was set for medical school but Georgina didn't mind for she, too, had set her sights on a medical career and when her schooling was finished she would start nursing training. . .

Suddenly Georgina jumped, jolted from the pleasant world of her daydreams back to the present, as she realised to her horror that Richard Fleetwood had said something to her, that they had all turned and were apparently waiting for her reply—and that she hadn't a clue what the question had been.

It was Andrew who came to her rescue. Andrew who knew her so well that probably, damn him, he even knew what she had been thinking.

'I think,' he said, 'Mr Oakley's observation chart is in the nurses' station, isn't that so, Staff Nurse?'

'Oh, yes, yes,' she muttered. 'I'll go and get it.' Thankfully she fled, away from Richard Fleetwood's questioning gaze, away from Neil Baltimore who was probably thinking she was some sort of imbecile, away from Heather Oakley's slightly bovine stare but, above all, away from Andrew's knowing look.

CHAPTER FOUR

THE following day when Georgina picked up the girls after she'd finished work her friend Jeanne—at whose house they had been—informed her that Natasha had been complaining of a sore throat.

'Oh no, not again,' said Georgina. 'That's all we need at the moment.'

'It's probably only a cold,' said Jeanne. 'Daisy had one last week. I expect she's caught it from her.'

'It might be,' agreed Georgina, 'but it's more likely to be another ear infection. Natasha's always been prone to them. If it is she'll need an antibiotic.' She glanced anxiously at her watch. 'I wonder if I could catch the surgery now.'

'Phone from here, if you like,' said Jeanne, pointing to her telephone.

'Thanks. I will. But I'd better have a look at Natasha first and make sure she wasn't having you on.'

'Is that a possibility?' Jeanne grinned.

'Let's just say it has been known,' replied Georgina darkly.

'She's upstairs with the others,' said Jeanne.

A swift word with her younger daughter and an examination of her throat and ears convinced Georgina that a visit to the surgery was indeed necessary. After making her phone call, she called up the stairs to tell Natasha to hurry and put her coat on.

'Did you get an appointment?' Jeanne came out into the hall as Natasha came clattering down the stairs.

'They're tacking us onto the end of the emergency surgery,' said Georgina. 'We've to see Dr Wooldridge's locum—a Dr Phillips, I think they said his name was.'

'Oh, yes,' said Jeanne. 'Isn't Dr Wooldridge away or something?'

Georgina nodded. 'Yes, a sabbatical, I believe.'

'Fancy word for a long holiday,' sniffed Jeanne.

'Nice work if you can get it.' Georgina nodded then, turning her attention to Natasha, urged her to hurry up as the surgery staff wouldn't wait for her if she was late. Leaving Lauren playing with Jeanne's children, they hurried outside to Georgina's car where she bundled Natasha into the back and instructed her to fasten her seat belt. Moments later she was on her way to Shalbrooke for the second time that day.

It was a clear bright evening with every sign of another frost to come.

'The stars are out already,' said Natasha from the back seat. 'I like coming out in the evenings. It's a bit like magic, isn't it, Mummy?'

'Yes, darling, it is,' agreed Georgina somewhat absent-mindedly as she approached Shalbrooke.

'Did you see Daddy today?' asked Natasha after a while.

'Yes. I see him every day,' Georgina replied.

She realised her mistake as Natasha said, 'It's not fair. I don't see Daddy every day. I wish I could. Why can't I see him every day, Mummy?'

'It's not possible, darling. I only see him because we work in the same place—you know that.'

Natasha was silent for a moment but as they passed the brightly lit hospital building she said, 'I still don't think it's fair. Jodie Michaels sees her daddy all the time.'

'But Jodie's daddy lives with her, doesn't he?' said Georgina, wishing somehow they could get off the subject. She would return to it later if that was what Natasha wanted but right at this moment there were other things to consider, like where she was going to park the car.

'I wish our daddy lived with us.' Natasha's voice had taken on a whining note. 'Why can't he, Mummy?'

'You know why, darling,' replied Georgina. 'We've talked about this lots of times.'

She managed at last to find a space in the Fleetwood Centre's car park, which was still surprisingly full in spite of the lateness of the hour. When they entered the centre they found the reason was that, although the main surgeries of the day were almost over, the group's female partner, Dr Kate Chapman, was conducting a Well Woman Clinic.

The receptionist assumed that Georgina had come to this clinic and when she told her that she had brought Natasha as an extra on the emergency surgery the girl glanced at the appointment book, then told them to go straight into one of the consulting rooms.

'Dr Phillips is waiting for you,' she said, her tone faintly disapproving as if they were deliberately late.

The locum was a giant of a man, blond, bearded, gentle and softly spoken.

'I hope we haven't kept you waiting,' said Georgina slightly breathlessly, 'but I've only just found out that Natasha has a sore throat. With her history of ear infections, I thought it best to bring her this evening rather than wait until tomorrow.'

'Did this come on suddenly or was it sore when you woke up this morning?' Dr Phillips asked Natasha.

'It was a bit sore this morning,' said Natasha.

'You didn't say,' said Georgina, staring at her.

'You were in a hurry,' said Natasha. 'Lauren said best not to—that it would make you late for work.'

Georgina bit her lip and Dr Phillips raised his eyebrows. 'The trials of a working mother?' he said, but he didn't sound unsympathetic.

'I've only been working for three days,' muttered Georgina.

He didn't comment but simply carried on examining Natasha's throat and ears. Straightening up, he said, 'You were quite right not to leave it until the morning. She does indeed have the start of an ear infection. I'll prescribe an antibiotic.'

He walked to his desk, and sat down and, after glancing through Natasha's notes, began to type out a prescription on the desk computer. While he was waiting for it to print he glanced up at Georgina. 'So, where do you work?' he said.

'Next door at the Shalbrooke,' she replied.

'Are you a nurse?' he asked, and there was no mistaking the interest in the question.

Georgina nodded, but before she could say more Natasha interrupted.

'Mummy's a staff nurse,' she said proudly.

'Is that so?' Dr Phillips smiled. 'Which department?'

'A and E,' replied Georgina.

'With Daddy,' breathed Natasha.

Dr Phillips raised his eyebrows. 'Your husband works there also?'

'He's Casualty Officer,' replied Georgina, taking the prescription that Dr Phillips handed to her. 'And he's my ex-husband,' she added.

'Really?' Even if she'd failed to notice his interest he'd shown when he'd learned she was a nurse, there was no mistaking his interest now as he learned she was unattached. Suddenly Georgina felt herself grow flustered under his gaze. She was totally out of touch with male appreciation and didn't know how to handle it. 'No doubt our paths will cross again, Mrs Merrick,' he said as he stood up, walked to the door and opened it for her.

'Maybe,' she replied as she hustled Natasha from the room. 'Thank you for seeing us, Dr Phillips.'

'My pleasure,' he replied.

The cold, frosty air hit their cheeks as they stepped

outside into the car park. 'Pull your scarf up over your mouth,' Georgina said to Natasha as they walked to the car. ·

'Mummy,' said Natasha wistfully as Georgina slipped the key into the keyhole, 'can I go and see Daddy?'

'Oh, I don't think so, darling,' she replied quickly. 'We need to get you home into the warm.'

'Please, Mummy, just for a minute. . .'

'We have to get your prescription and then we have to collect Lauren. . .' Georgina opened the car door and waited for Natasha to climb into the back seat.

'It seems awful,' said Natasha in the same wistful tone, 'that I'm here and Daddy is just over there and I can't see him. Look, I can even see the door and he's just on the other side. Think how upset he'll be when he knows I was right here and he couldn't see me.'

Georgina hesitated and as Natasha looked pleadingly up at her she saw the gleam of tears in her daughter's eyes.

'Please, Mummy, please. . .'

'Oh, all right.' She sighed, knowing her daughter had won. 'I don't suppose they'll mind if we leave the car here for a minute or two. . .and that's all it'll be, Natasha, just a minute or two.'

'Goody!' Her tears miraculously gone Natasha skipped alongside Georgina as they hurried through the car park and into the hospital grounds.

As they entered A and E Reception the first person they saw was Andrew. He was standing at the desk in the nurses' station, talking to Elliot. Both men looked up in surprise as they approached.

'Daddy!' called Natasha.

'Hello, poppet. Whatever are you doing here?' There was no mistaking Andrew's delight, then his gaze flew to Georgina. 'Is there anything wrong?' he asked quickly.

'No.' She shook her head. 'At least nothing too drastic.

Natasha has an ear infection. We've just been to the surgery to get a prescription and—'

'I wanted to see you,' Natasha interrupted.

'Quite right, too,' said Andrew solemnly, his gaze meeting Georgina's. 'I would have been most upset if you hadn't come in.'

'I told you so.' Natasha threw a triumphant look at her mother and Georgina sighed and looked away.

'So, what's all this about about bad ears?' Andrew had turned his attention back to Natasha.

'They are really bad,' said Natasha. 'And my throat,' she added for good measure. 'It's been really sore all day.'

'So, where have you been today?'

'With Aunty Jeanne.' She gave a huge sigh. 'Really, I suppose I should have been in bed. . .but Mummy had to go to work.'

'Well, yes, maybe you should. . .' Andrew began, but Georgina interrupted him.

'Don't you start,' she said sharply. 'I've just had the accusing bit from the doctor. If you think Natasha should be in bed when she gets an ear infection next time I'll send for you to look after her.'

'Will you?' squealed Natasha in delight. 'Just wait until I tell Lauren. She'll be dead jealous.'

'How is Lauren?' Andrew looked down at his daughter again, obviously choosing to ignore Georgina's comments.

'She's all right,' said Natasha in faint disgust. 'It's me what's ill.'

'Who's ill,' corrected Georgina automatically, 'not what's ill.'

'So, who did you see at the centre?' asked Andrew. 'I gather Paul Wooldridge is away.'

'Yes.' Georgina nodded. 'We saw his locum, a Dr Phillips.'

'He had a beard,' said Natasha, 'a golden beard.'

'Did he now?' Andrew chuckled and, looking back at Georgina, he said, 'Are you coming to the New Year's Eve staff party?'

'If I can arrange for someone to look after the girls I will. . . It's not easy to find anyone on that night. Everyone is involved in their own celebrations. . .unless, of course. . .' she paused and threw Andrew a speculative glance '. . .you'd like to have them.'

She saw him hesitate, as if he was desperately trying to find the right words in front of Natasha so as not to hurt her.

'Well,' he said at last, 'the thing is, I—'

She cut him short. 'It's all right, Andrew. Don't panic. I wasn't really going to ask you. I know you'll have made your own arrangements.'

'I shall only be coming here to the party,' he protested.

'I know,' she said softly. 'That's what I meant.'

It rained on New Year's Eve. Georgina was due to do a late afternoon shift and was on an early the next day.

'I shall probably live to regret this,' she said to her mother when she arrived with the girls at her house in Luccombe, where they would be staying for the night. 'I'm not used to partying any more.'

'It'll do you good,' said her mother. 'You should get out more, Georgina.'

'That's easier said than done,' replied Georgina. 'What with the girls to look after and now with my job, I don't seem to have much energy left for socialising.'

'How is the job going?' her mother, Lorna, asked after a moment. They were sitting in the conservatory of her home, watching the two girls as they played amongst the bare hydrangea bushes. In summer the bushes would blaze a trail of pinks and blues right down the pathway to the sea but now, on a damp winter's day, they looked sad and rather forlorn. It had stopped raining but the water still dripped from the branches of the trees that enclosed the garden.

'It's fine,' Georgina replied, resting her head briefly against the padded cane of the chair she was sitting in. 'Better than I'd feared.'

'You mean because of Andrew being there?' Her mother glanced sharply at her.

'Partly because of that, I suppose, and partly because of having been away from nursing for so long. . .and leaving the girls. . .oh, I don't know. . .lots of reasons, really. . .and I must confess I hadn't bargained for Andrew's girlfriend working on the same unit as well.'

'His girlfriend?' There was a startled pause. 'You don't mean. . .?'

'No, Mum, I don't mean that girlfriend. She hightailed it back to the mainland a long time ago—when she knew she was being cited, I believe. No, not her. This is another girl. . .a very young girl. . .too young for Andrew, according to Lauren. But, then, if it was left to Lauren I don't suppose anyone would be right for her father.'

'Except for you,' said her mother quietly.

'Except for me,' Georgina agreed.

There was another lengthy silence, during which they continued to watch the girls as they went on with their game. It was her mother who finally broke that silence.

'Georgina,' she said, and Georgina felt herself stiffen, recognising the tone of her voice. 'You don't think. . .?'

'No, Mum,' she said swiftly. 'I don't think. . .'

'Ah, well, never mind. I just wondered, that's all.'

'There's no point in wondering.' It came out far more sharply than she had intended and, catching sight of her mother's expression, Georgina let her breath out in a long sigh. 'I'm sorry,' she said a moment later. 'I didn't mean to snap. It's just that. . . Oh, I don't know, really.' She paused. In the distance they could hear the screams of hungry gulls as they swooped and dived for food but, apart from that, the garden was silent, with even the girls quiet now. 'I know you adored Andrew,' she went on at last, 'and that you think I was wrong for not giving him a second chance...but I couldn't. He hurt me so much. He destroyed everything we had...'

'Not everything,' said her mother quietly. 'You still have the girls.'

'It wasn't enough,' said Georgina passionately. 'Oh, I'm not saying it was all Andrew's fault. I've thought about it a lot just lately. I couldn't at first but I've forced myself to face the question as to why Andrew felt the need for an affair in the first place.'

'Did you reach any conclusions?' asked Lorna quietly.

'Only that it was at a time when he was under a lot of stress with his career and I was desperate to return to work. Maybe I went on about it too much. Andrew never wanted me to go back, you know that, and I tried to compromise, I really did. I was prepared to wait until Natasha started school...I suppose things became strained between us...but I still don't see that it gave him the right to do what he did.'

'And you don't feel able to forgive him? Not even now after all this time?'

'I couldn't stand the betrayal,' said Georgina passionately. 'I knew I would never be able to trust him again... Oh, I know you don't understand,' she said bitterly, throwing her mother a sharp glance, 'but, then, I couldn't really expect you to. Daddy was such a sweetie that he would never in a million years have put you through anything like this...' She trailed off.

Her mother opened her mouth as if to say something, then closed it again and they lapsed into silence once more, a silence which this time wasn't broken until the girls ran up the garden and erupted into the conservatory to show them some unusually shaped stones they had found.

An hour later Georgina left the house in Luccombe and drove down into nearby Shanklin, passing the little church in the old village where she and Andrew had been married twelve years before. It had all been so different then, she thought with a deep pang.

On a sudden impulse she drew off the road and switched off the car's engine. She sat with her arms resting on the steering-wheel, gazing through the damp greyness to the lych-gate and up the pathway to the church.

The contrast could hardly have been greater, she thought. It had been a day in early summer, heady with the scent of blossom, when family and friends had gathered to share her and Andrew's happiness. There had been laughter, sunshine and flowers, and there had been promises, too. Promises to love, to honour and to cherish.

On a second impulse she got out of the car and walked across the lane towards the church, passing under the pointed roof of the lych-gate and on up the flagstoned pathway between dark yews and crazily tilting gravestones which appeared to defy the laws of gravity. She half expected the church to be locked—most were in these days of vandalism—but, to her surprise, when she turned the ring handle and pushed, the huge door swung open.

If it was possible, it struck her as being even colder inside the building, and within seconds the raw damp seemed to strike into her very bones. She shivered and wondered why she had come in but then, compelled by the same impulsive urge as before, walked slowly up the aisle to the communion rail.

On that other day when she had made that same short walk to the altar her beloved father had been proudly by her side, and instead of wearing dark brown cords and a thick sweater she had worn wild silk and seed pearls. These same pews, empty now and slighty dusty, had been polished and full of people in unaccustomed finery, all turning slightly to smile as she approached.

Andrew had turned and smiled, too, and afterwards he had told her that his breath had caught in his throat at his first sight of her, the emotion threatening to choke him so that he feared he would be unable to say his vows. But he had said them. Had vowed to love her and, forsaking all others, keep her only unto himself as long as they both lived.

And as she stood there in the shadows on that dark winter's day Georgina's breath caught in her throat as she recalled the broken promises and shattered dreams.

She shouldn't have gone in there, she told herself angrily as she drove away from the church. She might have known it would only upset her. It was all her mother's fault, with her unspoken suggestion that she and Andrew might get together again. It had been a ridiculous notion. She knew it and her mother knew it and should have known better.

It began to rain again as she left Shanklin behind and headed inland, a persistent driving rain that lashed the windscreen, adding to her sense of depression.

Because of what had gone before, working alongside Andrew that day proved more difficult than usual, not that he, of course, was aware of what had happened or of the painful memories which had been evoked. In fact, the mood on A and E that day was full of festive anticipation and in direct contrast to Georgina's own.

'There are a lot of people coming,' said Dot during a lull in patients as she and Georgina stopped to chat. 'I think word must have got round after last year's bash just how good it was.'

'Do we have a live band?' asked Georgina, desperately trying to show some interest.

'Get real!' spluttered Dot. 'We're not made of money. Not that we wouldn't like one,' she added after a moment's reflection. 'But, no, we have to make do with Pete and Dave's Mobile Disco.'

Georgina's spirits sank even further. She'd never really been a disco person, at least not since her teens and then she had always gone with Andrew.

'They're very good, really,' Dot said, and Georgina forced herself to concentrate on what she was saying and at least look as if she was interested. 'They mix up the music very well to suit all tastes—you know, Golden Oldies, Sixties revivals and all that.'

'When you say Pete and Dave, do you mean our Pete and Dave—the paramedics?'

'Of course,' Dot laughed. 'It started years ago, apparently, when the disc jockey didn't turn up and the pair of them stepped in and made a better job of it. Since then they've been greatly in demand and they always oblige if they aren't on duty. . .' She trailed off as Helen suddenly looked round the corner of the nurses' station.

'Are you two still with us?' she asked, raising her eyebrows.

'Yes. Sorry, Helen.' It was Georgina who answered, at the same time smoothing down her uniform and adjusting her belt. 'Dot was just telling me what to expect tonight. Now, where would you like us?'

'Dot to the treatment room, please,' Helen replied. 'And you, Georgie, to cubicle three, please. A young woman with abdominal pain.'

Georgina hurried to the cubicles, pleased that it was Dot going to the treatment rooms and not herself. There was much more likelihood of working with Andrew there than there was on walking wounded. She had begun to pride herself that it no longer bothered her to work so closely with Andrew, but that had been before that morning and her ill-chosen visit to the church.

The woman with abdominal pain was already lying on the examination bed in the cubicle. She was in her early twenties and looked pale and drawn with pain, her dark hair damp with perspiration and her eyes wide with fear. She was accompanied by a man a good deal older than herself, whom Georgina took to be her father.

'I understand you are in a lot of pain.' Georgina smiled down sympathetically at the girl who nodded, then gritted her teeth as another spasm shook her thin body. 'I would like to do a few checks, if I may,' Georgina went on. 'Blood pressure, pulse rate—that sort of thing—then ask you a few questions and fill in some details. After that a doctor will come and see you.'

'Is all this really necessary?' It was the man who spoke. He sounded impatient. 'Can't we just get on with it? It's obvious that Wendy is in a great deal of pain. The pain is low down on her right side and even to a medically untrained person like myself I would say that suggests appendicitis—wouldn't you?'

'That's certainly a possibility,' said Georgina calmly as she set up a sphygmomanometer and secured the cuff on the girl's arm, 'but it's not the only consideration.'

The man fell silent and sat down on the one chair in the cubicle, gnawing the side of his thumb and watching while Georgina carried out and noted her observations.

The girl's pulse and blood pressure were above normal and her temperature was slightly raised, and when Georgina questioned her she admitted to a feeling of nausea.

'I just need to complete a few more details before the doctor comes.' Georgina turned to the front of the forms on which she was working. 'Your name is Wendy Mills and you are twenty-three. Is that correct?' When the girl, who had her eyes closed, wearily nodded in reply Georgina went on, 'Are you married, Wendy?'

Again the girl shook her head.

'So, who would be your next of kin?' Georgina glanced questioningly at the man who had looked up sharply. When Wendy remained silent she went on, 'Is it you?'

'No, no,' he said abruptly, 'it isn't me. I'm. . .I'm just a friend, that's all. I suppose her next of kin would be her mother. . .isn't that right, Wendy?'

The girl nodded, without opening her eyes.

'That's Janet,' the man muttered. 'Janet Mills.' He went on to give a Cowes address and Georgina dutifully wrote it onto the girl's record.

Glancing up again, she said, 'I need a few more details about the pain, Wendy. When exactly did it start?'

Behind her Georgina heard the man give an exasperated sound but Wendy herself opened her eyes. 'Late last night,' she said. 'It's gradually got worse and worse through the morning. . .' She stiffened, tensing her body as yet another spasm took over.

'Is there any chance you could be pregnant, Wendy?' asked Georgina when the pain obviously eased and the girl relaxed again.

'Oh, for goodness' sake!' The man almost exploded. 'Is all this really necessary? Can't we just get on with it? Wendy is obviously in great pain and needs some sort of treatment. We've been here for nearly an hour now. When the hell do we get to see a doctor?'

'Very soon,' Georgina replied. 'But, as you so rightly observed, Wendy needs some sort of treatment and it is our job to establish exactly what that treatment should be. You would hardly want us to whip her off to Theatre and perform an unnecessary operation just because we hadn't carried out the correct process of elimination, would you, Mr. . . Mr. . .? I'm sorry, I don't think I know your name,' she concluded.

'My name is immaterial to the situation,' the man muttered.

Georgina turned back to Wendy. 'So, tell me, Wendy, could you be pregnant?'

Wendy shot a look at the man but he had stood up and had turned his back to her. 'I'm not sure. . .' she whispered.

'When was your last period?' asked Georgina gently.

'I missed last month,' Wendy admitted at last.

The man swung round, glared at her and then, with another exasperated sigh, turned his back again.

'I'm sorry, Eric,' Wendy said, a pleading note in her voice. 'I was going to tell you. I really was. . .but. . .'

He turned again and looked at her—at the tears running down her cheeks—then his shoulders slumped and he moved to the other side of the bed where he took her hand. 'It's OK,' he muttered. 'Let's just get you sorted out, shall we?'

'I'll see if there's a doctor free.' Georgina stepped out of the cubicle, drawing the curtains behind her around the couple. Taking a deep breath, she made her way to the nurses' station. 'Helen,' she said as the sister looked up from a report she was writing. 'Is Susan Joliffe free?'

Helen shook her head. 'No, she's gone for her teabreak. Why, what have you got?'

'Possible ectopic, I think,' replied Georgina.

'Really? Well, here's Andrew—right up his street, I should say.'

'What's right up my street?' Andrew gave his lazy smile as he approached the desk.

'Gynae case. I always said you should specialise in Gynae,' said Helen. 'You've got the right bedside manner with the ladies.'

'Flattery will get you nowhere,' said Andrew. 'Now ask me properly and I might just take it on.'

'Dr Merrick, will you please move your butt to the cubicles and deal with a possible ectopic pregnancy,' snapped Helen.

'That's better.' Andrew grinned. 'I respond better to that sort of approach because it's what I'm used to.' He winked at Helen, then fell into step beside Georgina. 'Ectopic, you say?'

She nodded. 'Maybe. Low, right-sided pain, missed period.'

'Could be an ovarian cyst.'

'Yes, or appendicitis. . .but. . .'

'You'd plump for the pregnancy?'

'Yes, I think I would.'

'Any particular reason?' he asked as they approached the cubicle, and when Georgina hesitated he went on, 'Is she married?'

'No.'

'What age?'

'Twenty-three.'

'So, in a relationship. . .or a casual. . .?'

'It's a bit of an odd one. . .but see what you think. He looks old enough to be her father.' By this time they had reached the cubicle and Georgina whisked back the curtain.

Wendy Mills was alone.

'Oh.' For one moment Georgina was taken aback.

'Eric couldn't stay any longer,' said Wendy. 'He had to go. . .' She trailed off when she caught sight of Andrew.

'This is Dr Merrick, Wendy,' said Georgina. 'He's come to examine you.'

'Hello, Wendy.' Andrew picked up the notes that Georgina had made. 'I understand you are in a lot of pain.'

'Yes,' the girl nodded, then gasped again at a fresh onslaught.

'In that case,' said Andrew, 'I think it's high time we did something about it. First of all, I would like to examine you.'

As he carried out his examintion Georgina found herself remembering the times they had worked together in the past. She had always enjoyed working with Andrew, respecting both his skill and his judgement.

'I think this quite probably is an ectopic pregnancy,' he said at last, confirming Georgina's suggestion. 'Do you know what that is, Wendy?'

'Not really,' she said.

'It means that instead of growing in your womb the foetus is growing in one of your Fallopian tubes. This will eventually cause a dangerous situation.'

'So what are you going to do?' The girl looked frightened.

'First of all I'm going to get you moved up to a ward so that you can be examined by a gynaecologist. He will then arrange for you to go to Theatre and will answer any further questions you may wish to ask him. Now, is there anyone we can contact for you? Anyone you would like to be with you at this time?'

The girl shook her head and, catching Georgina's eye, she said, 'No, not Eric.'

'I was going to suggest your mother,' said Georgina.

'But she doesn't know. About any of this. About Eric. . . It'll be such a shock to her. . .' Wendy began to cry again.

Andrew took a large tissue from a box on the locker and handed it to her. Sitting on the bed, he said gently, 'I still think she would want to know—to be here with you. Now, you wipe your eyes and give Nurse here your mum's telephone number while I go and arrange a bed for you on the gynae ward.'

After he'd gone Wendy, still rather reluctantly, gave Georgina the number.

A little later Georgina returned to the cubicle, after making the call to the girl's mother, and found that Wendy had dried her eyes and, although still in great pain, seemed in a more positive frame of mind.

'What did my mum say?' she asked.

'Well, you were right, of course, about it being a shock to her to learn you were in hospital. She apparently thought you were at work. But she's coming straight to the hospital and bringing some things for you.'

'Did you tell her. . .about the pregnancy?'

Georgina shook her head. 'No, we don't know that for sure yet. I simply said you will probably be going to Theatre a little later today.'

'I see.' Wendy fell silent as Georgina began to tidy the equipment she'd used. After a while she said, 'He's married. Eric, I mean. That's why he couldn't stay. He doesn't want his wife to know about us, you see. . .'

I bet he doesn't, thought Georgina, but somehow she refrained from commenting.

'He's my boss,' Wendy went on after a moment. 'I don't know what will happen now. . .' Her eyes filled with tears again.

'If I were you,' said Georgina gently, 'I would try and rest for a while. Don't get upset and don't worry about tomorrow. All you have to do is concentrate on getting well again.'

Taking a deep breath, she made her way back to the nurses' station. Her shift was far from over but already she was beginning to think that when it was the last thing she felt like doing was going to a party to celebrate the New Year.

CHAPTER FIVE

GEORGINA went home to change before the party. The house seemed strange, oddly silent without the girls. She had no idea what she was going to wear. She went out so rarely these days that there hadn't seemed much point in buying party clothes. She pulled open her wardrobe door and stood for several moments, surveying the rack of clothes—most highly unsuitable for the type of function she was attending and geared more for trips to the stables with the girls, shopping or walks in the countryside.

Ever since she'd started work at the Shalbrooke the other female members of staff had relentlessly discussed what they would be wearing for the party. Most, it seemed, had indulged in something new. Well, she certainly hadn't—she would simply have to make do with one of her old dresses. At least no one will have seen them, she thought as she began to pull garments out from the back of the wardrobe. Except for Andrew, of course—he would have seen all of them because she most definitely hadn't splashed out on any new party gear since her divorce.

He'd seen the black, the one with the thin straps and the low back. That had been his favourite—he'd even helped her to choose it during a shopping trip to Southampton. She had bought it for an intimate dinner dance at a local hotel to celebrate their wedding anniversary.

Briefly she buried her face in the silky folds of the dress. Traces of her perfume still haunted the material and stirred memories so that for a moment she was back

71

there, dancing with Andrew on the hotel terrace in the heady scent of a moonlit summer's night. For one crazy moment she closed her eyes, imagining she could feel his arms around her and the touch of his cheek against hers.

So should this be the dress she should wear tonight? Opening her eyes, she hesitated and scanned the other clothes, her eye coming to rest at last on a scarlet dress in soft crushed velvet that she'd had for several years and had worn on numerous occasions—so numerous, in fact, that the actual events eluded her, unlike the occasion with the other dress.

Briefly she wondered what Denise White would be wearing. Some skimpy little number, no doubt, that showed more than it covered. Coming to a rapid decision, she bundled the black dress back inside the wardrobe and shook out the red one. She hung it on the wardrobe door while she went to shower.

When she was ready she phoned the girls to wish them goodnight.

'What are you wearing?' demanded Lauren.

'Oh, only that old red dress I've had for ages,' said Georgina.

'Dad liked that dress,' said Lauren.

'Did he?' Georgina said doubtfully.

'Yes,' Lauren replied. 'He used to call you Lady in Red. Don't you remember?'

'So he did,' she said, wondering if she had time to change into the black.

There was no time, however, and she doubted whether it was such a good idea anyway. After she'd spoken to Natasha and briefly to her mother, who told her to go and enjoy herself and not to worry about a thing, Georgina went to the front door of her cottage, where she waited for the staff minibus which was to pick her up and take her to the hospital social club.

*   *   *

She really hadn't wanted to go, and right up until the very last moment if there had been a justifiable excuse for getting out of it she would have seized it. But when she climbed out of the minibus, together with other nurses who had been picked up from the more outlying villages, and they were confronted by the lights of the club and snatches of music drifted towards them across the hospital grounds she was reminded of her carefree training days and she felt a sudden stab of excitement.

The dimly lit interior of the club had been fixed up with disco lights and by the time Georgina and her companions came out of the ladies' cloakroom, having deposited their coats, Dave Morey and Pete Steel had the proceedings well under way with a succession of vintage Abba and BeeGees records to get everyone in the right mood.

Georgina was quickly drawn into a group of her A and E colleagues, which included Elliot, Dot and Helen. Elliot bought her a drink and as she took a seat at their table she looked round at other groups who were assembling as more and more people crowded into the club and a few brave couples took to the dance floor.

Within minutes Georgina knew she had made a mistake and that she should have worn the black dress. There didn't appear to be another coloured dress in sight but there were black dresses of every shape and size. Short black dresses which exposed long Lycra-clad thighs and barely-covered bottoms, long black dresses that skimmed the floor or—trimmed with sequins or beads—covered ample bosoms. There were even black harem pants teamed with loose-sleeved blouses and fancy waistcoats—but no colours.

'You look fantastic.' Helen leaned across the table and spoke, raising her voice with difficulty above Robin Gibb's falsetto.

'I feel hopelessly out of date,' replied Georgina ruefully. 'I didn't realise black was the order these days.'

'It's ridiculous how we allow ourselves to be ruled by the fashion gurus,' snorted Helen. 'I'm not going to do it again. Next year I'm going to wear powder-blue. You look by far the most intriguing woman in the place.'

Georgina, who wasn't at all sure she wanted to intrigue anyone, found herself looking round again. There was no sign of Andrew yet. Not that she was looking for him, of course, just that she couldn't help noticing that he wasn't there. Denise White was there, she realised with a little shock as she caught sight of the petite blonde, talking to a group that included Susan Joliffe and a couple of junior housemen. She, predictably, was clad in the proverbial little black dress that seemed to consist more of straps than of dress, but she wasn't with Andrew. Georgina turned to speak to Helen again but quickly realised that her attention had been diverted by yet another group that had just arrived.

'It's the Fleetwood party,' Helen murmured, rising to her feet. 'I'd better go and ask them if they want to join us, especially as it was me who invited them in the first place.'

'She'll be happy now,' observed Dot as they watched Helen walk across the club to the entrance.

'Why's that?' asked Georgina innocently.

'Richard Fleetwood's here.'

'And that will make Helen happy?'

'Oh, yes.'

'Really? I didn't know.' Georgina was faintly surprised. She'd known Helen for a long time and she'd also known that Richard Fleetwood had been widowed a few years previously but she'd never connected the two.

'You just look at her face when they come back,' chuckled Dot. 'Let's see now, who else is here out of the Fleetwood mob? Oh, there's Kate Chapman and Elizabeth French, their practice manager. . . Oh, I say, who's the blond guy with the beard? Haven't seen him before.'

'Oh, I have,' said Georgina quickly. 'That's the locum, Dr Phillips. I saw him when I took Natasha to the surgery. He was very nice. . .' She trailed off, remembering the look she'd seen in his eyes when he'd learnt she was unattached.

'You can say that again,' said Dot. 'In fact, I would say very, very nice. . .' At that moment Norman Westfield, the A and E porter, approached their table, brandishing a book of raffle tickets. 'Oh, no, Norman, not again. I bought mine when I came in,' Dot protested. 'I'm not buying any more, even if the first prize is a romantic weekend for two.'

'It wasn't you I was after,' said Norman. 'It was your friend.'

'Story of my life.' Dot rolled her eyes as Georgina fumbled in her bag for some change.

'Thanks, love.' Norman grinned as he tore off a strip of tickets and handed them to Georgina. 'You won't regret it, I can assure you. And if you get the first prize you can take me with you.'

'Dream on, sunshine,' said Dot.

'So where is it, then, this romantic weekend?' Georgina laughed.

'Venice, no less,' said Norman, and after a quick rendition of 'O Sole Mio' moved on to the next table.

'Oh,' said Georgina, 'Venice.'

'Never been there myself,' said Dot. 'My sister went and thought it very overrated—you been?' she asked, turning to Georgina.

'Yes.' Georgina nodded. 'I've been. . .but it was a very long time ago.'

'Doubt it's changed much.' Dot gave a short laugh. 'Those sort of places don't. So what did you think of it?'

'I thought it was wonderful,' said Georgina.

'Oh, well, takes all types, I suppose. In that case, you'll be hoping to win first prize.'

'I don't know about that,' Georgina said dryly. 'Places are never the same when you return to them.' Especially, she added silently, when the first time was your honeymoon.

'So, we meet again.' While Georgina and Dot had been talking the Fleetwood group, together with Helen, had made their way to the table, and Dr Phillips had stopped before Georgina and was smiling down at her.

'Hello, Dr Phillips.' She smiled back. 'It's a small world.'

'So I'm finding out, and even smaller when it's an island world. . . And, please, it's Simon.' He slipped into the seat beside her, the seat where Helen had been sitting. Georgina threw her an apprehensive glance but Helen seemed pink, flushed and more than happy to be sitting alongside Richard Fleetwood while Elliot went off to the bar again to order more drinks.

'What else have you been finding out about us Islanders?' Georgina asked, turning back to Simon Phillips.

He considered for a moment, as if carefully weighing up her question, then he said, 'That you are, on the whole, welcoming and friendly to us overners. . .but that at the same time you are fiercely protective of your island and do not take kindly to criticism.'

'Why should we?' said Georgina lightly. 'Most people come here because they choose to, usually to get away from the pace of life on the mainland. Some then criticise what they find or try to change things to resemble what they wanted to escape from. I have to say I find that illogical.'

'Good point.' Simon gave a short laugh. 'Can I take it you are a dyed-in-the-wool Islander?'

'Born and bred,' she replied, 'and proud of it.'

'I can understand that,' he said, then added, 'it really is a beautiful place.'

'How long will you be here?' Georgina asked a little later, during a brief lull in the music while Dave Morey indulged in some good-natured banter with those on the dance floor and while, just for the moment, she didn't have to raise her voice.

'About three months,' Simon replied, looking up as Elliot arrived back at the table with a full tray and taking the glass of beer that was handed to him.

'I thought Paul Wooldridge had gone for a year.' Georgina frowned, wondering if she had been misinformed.

'He has. Cheers.' Simon took a sip of his beer and glanced round the table. Others, too, raised their glasses and responded. 'But I'm due to take up another appointment in the spring at a practice in Oxford so I'm only able to stay until then. I say. . .' he glanced up as the music started again '. . .do you fancy a dance? I love this sixties stuff.'

Georgina only hesitated for a moment before she got to her feet. Why not? she thought as Simon took her hand and led her onto the floor. After all, wasn't that why one came to a disco—to dance? And, as Simon had said, the sounds of the sixties and of Neil Sedaka were very persuasive.

For such a big man Simon Phillips was very light on his feet, and he quite obviously loved to dance. They stayed on the floor throughout the sixties revival, which ended with a lengthy Beatles medley, by the end of which Dave Morey had cajoled or shamed most people onto the floor. So as not to lose his audience, Dave switched the tempo to a slow, smoochy number, and as Whitney Houston told someone she would always love him Simon Phillips put his arms around Georgina and drew her close.

It had been a very long time since she'd been held by

a man and it felt strange, alien almost. She was used to
Andrew with his lean, hard body, his dark good looks and
his humour—more often than not a string of outrageous,
whispered comments that would leave her helpless with
mirth. And now here she was being held by another, a
man so different from Andrew that if she had set out to
choose one she couldn't have made a better job.

Tall, broad and fair, his embrace was almost like a
bearhug, his beard soft where Andrew's cheek was
smooth and clean-shaven. Even the scent of him was
different, some sharp citrus preparation where Andrew
used a musk-based aftershave. But more than that, the
male scent—the natural one designed to attract
females—was different. Not unpleasant, just different.

But why was she comparing him to Andrew? She
really had to stop that, she knew. She had to start living
again. Andrew was in the past. She had to move forward,
make new friends. . .perhaps find love again. She stiffened slightly as Simon held her even closer. Because of
the sheer size of him she could barely see over his shoulder but as he moved she realised with a slight sense of
shock that next to them was Andrew, and he was dancing
with Denise White.

For one long moment her gaze met Andrew's and,
with both their partners apparently oblivious to what was
happening behind their backs, neither she nor Andrew
seemed able to look away.

And suddenly, strangely, in the half-light—to the poig-
nant, familiar strains of the well-known song—it was as
if so much was summed up in that one moment—all
the excitement and happiness they had once shared, the
passion, the hopes and fears and the pain in the sorrow
of their parting.

Georgina felt a lump rise in her throat. Why had it
happened? How could it have all gone so wrong? As she
and Andrew continued to stare at each other in some

kind of dumb anguish Georgina found his image becoming blurred and knew she was seeing him through a mist of tears.

In the end Simon moved again, blocking her vision so that she could no longer see Andrew. But it was too late. The harm was done, and from that moment all she could see in her mind's eye was his arms around Denise, holding her close, his hand on the bare skin of her smooth back and his cheek against hers. Denise had been smiling. Georgina had seen that much in the brief moment before the girl had turned away. Had Andrew been murmuring something, some outrageous observation or suggestion that had made her smile, the way he used to do with her?

Suddenly Georgina could bear it no longer and with a murmured excuse she pulled away from Simon and they returned to their table.

She knew she shouldn't have come. Knew she would only be miserable, she told herself a little later as she escaped to the ladies' cloakroom and attempted to cool her burning cheeks. She couldn't even go home because she had to wait for the minibus to take her.

Eventually, with her make-up repaired, she took a deep breath and prepared to return to the fray. There was nothing else to do but pull herself together and make the best of it. After all, she told herself firmly, it couldn't last for ever.

When she returned to her table it was to find that Simon had bought her another drink and that Richard Fleetwood was waiting to dance with her. In fact, she was given no more time to feel sorry for herself for Simon, in spite of her protests, whisked her onto the floor for a rock 'n 'roll session after Richard, and after that Elliot claimed her for an uproarious Country and Western medley.

It took a while for everyone to recover from all the frenzy and once again the lights dimmed and couples became entwined as Phil Collins's familiar husky tones told about 'One More Night'.

For the moment Georgina was happy to sit in the corner and sip a long, cool, orange juice. Dot was dancing with Elliot, Helen with Richard and Simon with Kate Chapman so, briefly, she was alone. She could no longer see Andrew and she was thankful for that. She had no desire to watch him with Denise and was glad that he seemed to be keeping to the other end of the club, well away from her table. The others in her group had certainly ensured that she was having a better time than she had feared but she was still very much aware that aggravation only hovered a stone's throw away beyond the edges of the dimmed lights.

The others began to return to the table. Vaguely she heard Pete Steel say something over the PA system about a special request and then, as the notes of a familiar introduction floated across the room, she felt someone take her hand. Startled, she looked up to find Andrew at her side.

As if in a dream, she allowed him to raise her to her feet and in the same trance-like state and in front of all the other members of her group permitted him to lead her onto the floor. Then, while Chris de Burgh told everyone about his 'Lady in Red', Andrew drew her into his arms.

It felt exactly the same as it always had, and as the last months and years rolled away it was as if all the pain and heartache had never been. Neither of them spoke, just swayed slightly to the music, cheeks lightly touching. Then, as other couples took to the floor and crowded round them, Andrew spoke. And it was not a whispered endearment, nor was it an outrageous comment. Instead, quite calmly, he said, 'Have you bought a raffle ticket?'

'Have you?'

'Of course. It would be nice to return to Venice. Don't you agree?'

'Maybe,' she replied cautiously.

'What first springs to mind when you think of Venice?' he murmured.

She only hesitated for a second. 'The colour of the sea.' Her reply was light.

'And. . .?'

She pretended to consider. 'Gondolas on the Grand Canal. . .'

'At night, you mean, drifting in the moonlight to the strains of a Puccini aria?' There was amusement in his voice now and ever so slightly he tightened his grip.

'If you like.' Again she attempted coolness, a casual reply, but feared she was failing miserably.

They were silent for a few moments, then teasingly Andrew said, 'So aren't you going to ask me what memories I carry of Venice?'

'I wasn't, but I'm sure you'll tell me anyway.' It was becoming increasingly difficult to stay cool with him, but she knew if she encouraged him too much she would only live to regret it—even more than she already was.

'I think of early mornings behind cool shutters,' he murmured against her hair, 'of late-night suppers on a certain balcony. . .of a shared bottle of wine. . .of an old-fashioned bath, so big it was obviously meant for two. . . Yes, it would be good to return to Venice. . .'

'The company would be different and. . .and the circumstances. . .' Georgina struggled to keep her voice even, thrown by his references to the more intimate details of their honeymoon.

'So who would you take?' There was a note of questioning amusement in his voice.

'The question is purely hypothetical,' she replied lightly. 'I never win raffles.' She didn't ask who he would take because she didn't want to hear his reply—didn't even want to contemplate him and Denise White in Venice together.

'Maybe your new friend would like to go,' he murmured in her ear a moment later.

'My new friend. . .? Oh, you mean Simon,' she said. 'Yes, maybe he would.'

'Who is he exactly?'

Suddenly, as she realised that he didn't know and that the questioning note in his voice sounded ever so slightly like jealousy, Georgina realised she was beginning to enjoy herself. 'Simon Phillips,' she replied in the same light tone. 'He's Paul Wooldridge's locum.'

'Ah,' said Andrew. 'Natasha's man with the golden beard.'

Georgina nodded.

'How is Natasha?'

'Much better,' Georgina replied. 'We got the antibiotic in time.'

'Good.'

They fell silent again, listening to the words of the song. While they had been talking they had moved slightly apart but now he drew her close once more and his arms tightened around her.

Briefly Georgina forgot everyone else—Denise White, Simon Phillips—everyone except herself and Andrew as she allowed herself a rare moment of nostalgia. She knew that later she would probably regret it, but for the moment she was happy to allow this interlude just for old times' sake.

Then when it was almost over Andrew said, 'You look lovely tonight, Georgina—I always loved you in that dress.'

And quite suddenly the magic, elusive to start with, was over as inadvertently he reminded her that her dress was old, that she was different from the other women and that the in thing today was to wear black. As her earlier humiliation returned she felt dated, old-fashioned—right back there in the eighties, along with their relationship and the 'Lady in Red'. And if further endorsement of the fact were needed, the final strains of the song died away to be swiftly replaced by a modern hit from the charts by a group that Georgina had never heard of but a group whom everyone else seemed to know, if the way they surged forward onto the floor was anything to go by.

To Georgina's relief the raffle, drawn just before midnight, was won neither by herself nor Andrew but by one of the nursing managers. This caused a great deal of grumbling and muttering amongst the rest of the staff, with protests that the lady in question hardly needed the weekend break after the two foreign holidays she'd already taken in the last year.

Georgina was also relieved when midnight, with its chimes, kisses, poppers, streamers and its tear-jerking 'Auld Lang Syne' gave way to the hokey cokey, to be followed in rapid succession by 'Knees up Mother Brown' and the conga. She was not usually a party-pooper but she had spent too many previous New Years' Eves in Andrew's company to cope wholeheartedly with this one, where she was with him yet not with him.

Simon had claimed her as his partner as midnight had approached and now, as the crowd grew more wild and disorganised, he remained by her side as she looked on, wishing once more that she could go home.

'Not quite your scene, this part?' he said in her ear, raising his voice above the din.

'Not really,' she smiled, then added, 'At least, not this year.'

'Would you like another drink?'

'No, thank you. What I'd really like is to go home.'

'How are you getting home?'

'The minibus, but that's not coming until one o'clock.'

'Where do you live?' He had to yell this time to make himself heard as the conga line came round again and passed in front of them, with all the normally upright members of the medical staff shrieking and waving for them to join on the straggling line.

'Newtown,' she yelled back.

'Come on,' he said, setting his glass down on a table and taking her arm. 'I'll run you home.'

She followed him outside into the comparative quiet of the club's foyer. 'Did you bring your car?' she asked.

He nodded. 'Believe it or not, I'm on call. Someone has to be.' He grinned when he saw her expression. 'I've been incredibly lucky until now—I suppose most folk have been too busy enjoying themselves to think about being ill. Give it an hour or so and they'll all start to come round. And, don't worry,' he added as she began to walk to the cloakroom to get her coat, 'I've only had the one pint—the rest was Coke.'

Georgina didn't wait to argue—she was just relieved she didn't have to stay for what could be another hour at least by the time they'd got everyone rounded up and into the minibus.

Struggling into her coat, she joined Simon again in the foyer, and as he paused to help her the conga line began to wend its way through the doors.

'Come on, let's get out of here quick.' He took her hand and together they fled out of the building and across the car park to his car.

It wasn't until she was seated beside him in the darkness and they were hurtling through the deserted country lanes that the unusualness of the situation suddenly struck Georgina. She couldn't remember a time when she'd been alone in a car with a strange man, especially at that time of night. In fact, she thought, allowing herself a surreptitious glance at Simon's profile, she probably never had—except with Andrew. Not that she need have any fears about Simon, of course—he was a doctor after all.

'I enjoyed that,' said Simon. 'It's a long time since I had a dance and I must say they mixed the music very well.'

'Yes, I agree,' Georgina replied. 'It's a long time for me, too, since I've been to a disco. I tend to enjoy classical music more these days.'

They continued to discuss each other's tastes in music until at last Georgina said, 'You need to take the next turning to the right. I live over there,' she added as he carried out the turn, 'in one of those cottages.'

'What a charming spot,' he said as he drew up at the gate she indicated. 'At least it looks it in the moonlight. I suppose it is in the daytime as well?'

'Yes, it is.' She turned, slightly dismayed as he switched off the engine. She had been prepared to simply thank him for the lift and go indoors. It seemed that Simon had other ideas.

'Can't go waking the neighbours,' he said.

'No,' she agreed, then fell silent, desperately trying to think of something witty to say but failing miserably. What was she supposed to do now? Did he expect her to ask him in—give him coffee at this time of night? She really was quite useless when it came to this sort of thing. She knew in her heart that she didn't want to ask him in. She liked him, had enjoyed his company that evening and was grateful for the lift home but she was truly tired and wanted nothing more than to fall into bed and sleep.

She had to be on duty the following morning, then she had to pick the girls up from her mother's and, if all that wasn't enough, she was due to take them to the pantomime in the evening. Surely Simon wasn't expecting her to ask him in?

'Was that your ex-husband you were dancing with?'

Simon spoke suddenly, almost making her jump.

'Er...yes,' she replied. 'Yes, that was Andrew.'

'I thought perhaps it was.' He paused and Georgina wondered what was coming next. 'You're still on good terms, then?'

'Reasonably good, yes. But we have to be because of the girls.'

'Not all divorced couples are.'

'No, I suppose not.' Another silence followed and Georgina was almost on the point of telling Simon how tired she was when unexpectedly he said, 'I was wondering... Perhaps you'd like to come out with me one evening.'

'Well... I...' Taken by surprise, she hardly knew what to say.

'Nothing high-powered...a drink, maybe?'

'That's kind of you, Simon. I—' She was saved from committing herself further as his pager suddenly went off.

'I thought it was too good to be true,' he muttered, unclipping the mobile phone from the dashboard.

'That was Amubulance Control,' he said a moment later. 'I have to go. I'm sorry, Georgina.'

'That's all right, Simon.' She hoped she didn't sound too relieved. 'I must go in, anyway.'

'Think about what I said.' He smiled as he helped her from the car, then shut the door.

'I will, and thank you, Simon.' She watched as he drove off into the night and with a little sigh she turned and let herself into the cottage.

She'd taken her coat off and was about to go upstairs to bed when she heard a car door slam, followed almost immediately by a knock on her front door. Her heart sank. Simon had returned. Maybe she'd left something in his car. Without stopping to think further, she opened the door—to find Andrew standing on the doorstep.

CHAPTER SIX

'ANDREW!' Georgina stared at him in astonishment. The collar of his dark jacket was turned up against the cold of the night and there was a frown on his face. 'Whatever's the matter?' Automatically and without hesitation Georgina found herself standing aside to allow him into the cottage.

'Are you alone?' he muttered, prowling through the tiny hallway and peering first into the sitting room and then through the crack of the door into the kitchen.

'Of course I'm alone. The girls are with Mum. What is this, Andrew, what's wrong?'

'I wanted to make sure you'd got home safely.' He was still muttering but the uncharacteristic scowl which had been on his face when she'd opened the door was slowly being replaced by a rather sheepish look of embarrassment.

'Why should you be worried about me getting home safely?' Georgina led the way into the kitchen.

'I thought you were going home in the minibus with the other girls,' he said, 'then I heard someone say that you'd already gone. I was a bit concerned, that's all.'

'Well, I appreciate your concern, Andrew.' She gave a short laugh. 'But I can assure you it was totally unnecessary. As you can see, I'm here safe and sound.' Her eyes narrowed slightly. 'But what about you? How did you get here?'

'I drove,' he said shortly.

'But haven't you been drinking?'

He shook his head. 'I'm on the early shift so I laid off the booze tonight.'

'Oh.' She stared at him for one moment, not knowing quite what to say, and then, when it seemed that he was not about to offer any further information, she said, 'Well, now that you're here you'd better have a coffee.' Turning to the worktop, she took the kettle to the sink and filled it while Andrew leaned against the fridge and watched her.

She took two mugs from the cupboard and spooned instant coffee into them, automatically adding sugar to Andrew's. 'So, don't you want to know how I did get home?' she asked him after a moment. When he remained silent she looked over her shoulder at him. Knowing Andrew as she did, one look at his face told her what she needed to know.

'You know, don't you?' she said accusingly. The kettle boiled at that moment and she turned back to the worktop to fill the mugs.

'Know what?' He tried to sound nonchalant but failed miserably.

'How I got home. You know Simon Phillips bought me.' She handed Andrew his coffee and picked up her own, curling her hands around it as if drawing comfort from its warmth. Again Andrew remained silent. 'And, before you ask,' she went on a second later, 'he hadn't had much to drink either because he was on call for the Fleetwood Centre so, you see, you needn't have worried—I was perfectly safe.'

Still Andrew didn't comment and they sipped their coffee in silence. Then Georgina said, 'I'm on an early tomorrow as well, that is, if I can get up—I'm not used to late nights any more. I thought Simon was going to want to come in for coffee. I must admit I was quite relieved when he didn't. And now here I am staying up and drinking coffee with you.'

She expected Andrew to laugh, to see the irony of the situation. But he didn't. Instead the frown was back on his face. 'So, who is he exactly, this Phillips character?' he muttered at last, scowling into the depths of his mug.

Georgina stared at him. 'You know who he is. He's Paul Wooldridge's locum.'

'And that tells us what? Precisely nothing.' He paused, then relentlessly he went on, 'You don't know him from Adam, Georgina, and yet you got into his car in the early hours of the morning and allowed him to drive you home through deserted country lanes to an empty cottage. Honestly, for a moment there, I thought you must have taken leave of your senses.'

'For goodness' sake, Andrew.' She put her mug down onto the worktop and stared at him in disbelief. 'I think it's you who has taken leave of your senses, not me. Simon is perfectly respectable and a thoroughly nice guy, and surely you're forgetting the most important factor?'

'What's that?'

'He is a doctor, just in case it had escaped your notice.'

'You could say that was sufficient enough cause for concern,' he muttered darkly.

'For God's sake, Andrew, what's that supposed to mean?'

He shrugged. 'Not a lot. Simply recalling some of the medical students I trained with, that's all. Presumably they, too, are doctors now but I wouldn't trust them as far as I could throw them—'

'Oh, so that's what this is all about. Jealousy, is that it? It had nothing to do with drink driving or being attacked—'

'Oh, come on, Georgina, you're being silly now.'

'Am I? Am I?' She could hear her voice beginning to rise to a shrill, unattractive pitch but could do nothing to stop it. 'You thought he was here, didn't you, Andrew?' she demanded. 'When you came in just now you thought Simon was here. That's why you were prowling around. So what would you have done if he had been? Asked him if his intentions towards your ex-wife were perfectly honourable? Is that what you had in mind?'

'Now you really are being ridiculous. . .' Andrew was beginning to look shamefaced.

'Really? So you're saying you wouldn't have minded. Is that it? Well, for your information, and I can't really see why I'm telling you because it really isn't any business of yours any longer, Simon has asked me to go out with him.'

Andrew's eyes narrowed. 'Will you go?'

'Probably. Maybe. I don't know. Would it bother you if I did?'

He didn't answer and she continued to stare at him. 'It would, wouldn't it, Andrew?' she said at last.

'Honestly,' she went on when he stayed silent, 'you're the absolute limit.' With an exasperated gesture she turned away. 'It's OK for you to play around, to have relationships, but when it comes to me it's another matter, isn't it?' She paused questioningly but still he remained silent. 'Well, I tell you now, Andrew—' sharply she swung back to face him '—it was you who messed things up, not me. I have the rest of my life to get on with and I don't see why I should spend that alone. Neither do I see that I should seek your permission every time I want to—' She broke off with a sound in her voice suspiciously like a sob.

'Georgina, please.' Andrew took a tentative step towards her. He set his mug down and, taking her by her shoulders, drew her towards him. 'Please,' he murmured again, this time against her hair and, it seemed, almost desperately.

For a long moment they remained where they were, perfectly still, with neither of them speaking.

Then gently, very gently, he put one hand beneath her

chin and, tilting her face towards him, he gazed down into her eyes.

Georgina felt powerless to move, as if the events of the evening had somehow rendered her helpless. Even when she felt his lips cover hers, in a kiss so familiar it was almost like breathing, she remained still.

How easy it would be to respond, to give in. To allow him not only to kiss her but to take her upstairs, to undress her and to make love to her—and so thoroughly that it would dispel that ache deep inside her, that ache which during the last few months had become so permanent she had begun to despair that it would ever go away.

The conditions were right—they were quite alone in the cottage, without even the girls to ask awkward questions or to jump to impossible conclusions.

Would it matter? Just this once? No one would know, and if anyone did would they care? Who was there to care? The girls? They would be delighted. Her mother? She, too, would welcome Andrew back into the fold with open arms if she thought there was any chance of a reconciliation. What of Simon Phillips? What of him? Andrew had been quite right when he'd said she hardly knew him. He hardly came into the equation. Denise White, then—what of her?

Abruptly she drew away from Andrew. She'd been down that road before, only last time it hadn't been Denise White—it had been another woman, a woman who had caused her untold pain and anguish. But now it was Denise. She couldn't even contemplate putting herself in such a position again. She'd survived last time. She doubted she would a second time.

'I think you'd better go, Andrew,' she said abruptly.

Sharply he drew in his breath and with a deep sigh he said, 'Yes, I guess I had. If that's what you want, Georgina.'

'Yes,' she said shakily, repeating more firmly, 'yes, Andrew, it is.'

The early morning shift of New Year's Day more often than not was a difficult one. Staff were hungover and tired from the previous night's celebrations, while patients could be aggressive and not prepared to make any allowances.

Helen Turner stood at the desk in the deserted nurses' station and scrutinised the staff rota. She, too, was tired. It had been very late when she had at last got to bed, and during the night she had been up twice to help her father. He had got distressed because she had gone out for the evening and left him with a sitter, and so when he awoke he could not be reassured that she wouldn't be going out again.

Helen sighed as she recalled the ensuing scenes and wearily pushed a stray strand of her fair hair inside her cap. Her social life these days was almost non-existent as her father's Alzheimer's disease progressed. And, if she was honest, there were some days when she was so tired she didn't know how she got through, let alone coped with the demands of her job. The organisation that had been required to allow her to attend last night's festivities had been quite exhausting—but, she thought with a little smile, it had all been worth it.

The party had been a great success. Dave Morey and Pete Steel had excelled themselves, people had attended from every department in the hospital and in the end almost the entire workforce from the Fleetwood Centre had turned up. Even Richard, she thought, and discos were certainly not his scene, not by any stretch of the imagination. . .

She looked down again at the staff list and saw that both Andrew and Georgina Merrick were on duty that morning. She hoped Georgina had enjoyed herself the night before. She had, Helen knew, been a bit reluctant to come but she certainly hadn't been short of partners, which was hardly surprising for Georgina really was a very attractive woman and in her red dress had looked quite stunning. She seemed to have scored with that new locum from the Fleetwood Centre and at one point Helen had seen her dancing with Andrew.

She sighed again. It really was such a shame about those two. They looked so perfect together and they'd had so much going for them. . .

Helen had been working with Andrew at the time of the break-up. She'd heard the whispers and rumours about his affair with a radiologist and had chosen to ignore them, hoping they weren't true. She'd known how devastated Georgina would be if she'd found out and had hoped she wouldn't—that the whole thing would simply fizzle out.

But Georgina had found out, enlightened by a well-meaning 'friend' who had thought she really ought to know what her husband was up to.

The affair had ended as abruptly as it had started, the radiologist had hightailed it back to the mainland where she had come from in the first place and Helen and the rest of the staff had hoped everything would get back to normal. After all, it was perfectly plain that it had only been a temporary infatuation on Andrew's part and that he was really devoted to Georgina and to his two girls.

Unfortunately, Georgina, devastated by events, hadn't seen it that way and within a few short months the Merricks had joined the divorce statistics. Helen had helplessly watched them fall apart. Andrew, devastated by what had happened, and Georgina, struggling to keep afloat for her daughters' sake.

Seeing the two of them dancing together last night had somehow brought it all back. . . Maybe, Helen thought, there was a chance that some spark had been rekindled.

She hoped so. Secretly she would like nothing better than to see the Merricks get back together again and make another go of their marriage.

She glanced up as the doors swung open and, as if on cue—as if she'd known she'd been the centre of Helen's thoughts—Georgina appeared. She looked not just tired, which would have been understandable, but drawn and with purple smudges beneath her dark eyes.

'You look like I feel,' Helen joked in an attempt to bring a smile to the pinched cheeks.

'I'm out of practice, simply not used to these late nights. . .' Georgina trailed off as Dot suddenly pushed open the doors.

If anything, she looked even worse than either Georgina or Helen.

'I'm never, ever going to drink Bacardi and Coke again. . .not ever. . .not ever again. . .' she muttered. She would have carried on walking zombie-fashion straight to the changing room without moving her head, but as she passed the other two she paused, then very slowly, very gently, she turned and looked at Georgina. 'What happened to you?' she said.

'What do you mean?' Georgina frowned but Helen noticed that her cheeks had reddened slightly.

'Last night—you just disappeared. The last time I saw you was when we were doing the conga, then later I realised you'd gone. The minibus lot were looking for you. They didn't want to go without you.'

'I had a lift home,' Georgina said. 'I didn't really want to stay till the end, and when I had the opportunity to leave I took it. I suppose I should have let the others know, really. I didn't think. . .'

'So who took you?' Dot was obviously dying with curiosity, in spite of her hangover.

'Was it Andrew?' asked Helen, watching Georgina closely and hoping that it might be so.

'No.' Georgina shook her head. 'No, it wasn't Andrew. Actually. . .it. . .it was Simon. . . Simon Phillips.'

Dot stared at her. 'You mean the locum guy?'

'Yes.' Georgina swallowed, then nodded.

'I don't know. . .' Dot rolled her eyes '. . .some people seem to get all the luck. He barely even glanced in my direction. You flutter your eyelashes at him and he takes you home.' Muttering to herself, she went off to the changing room.

Helen, still watching Georgina, had seen some other emotion enter the dark eyes, some emotion she found difficult to define. 'Are you all right?' she said gently, intuition telling her that there was much more to all this than Georgina was letting on.

Georgina glanced up. 'Oh, yes,' she said with forced casualness.' Yes, I'm fine.'

But a moment later, as the doors opened yet again and Andrew strode through, Georgina turned and, with her head down, she hurried off after Dot.

'Morning, Andrew.' Helen nodded and, although Andrew nodded back, she couldn't help but notice that his gaze was on Georgina's retreating figure. 'And how are you this morning?' she added. 'Did you also overdose on Bacardi?'

'No,' he said shortly and added, 'So at least I don't have a hangover to contend with, along with everything else.'

Helen watched him as he took himself off to the doctors' restroom and came to the conclusion that she had been right in her assumption that something had happened between Georgina and Andrew the previous night. She also had the feeling that Simon Phillips had in some way been involved but she had no time to speculate further for at that moment the first of the day's patients began to arrive.

*   *   *

Georgina didn't see Andrew again until later in the morning. If the truth were known, she had been feeling a bit guilty about her outburst of the night before. Maybe, she thought, she had jumped to conclusions about Andrew's motives for following her home by assuming that he had thought she had invited Simon into the cottage. Maybe he had quite simply been concerned about her. But if, on the other hand, he had been checking up on her, she told herself as she went about the morning routine, he quite simply had to learn that what she did these days, and with whom, was absolutely none of his business.

Finally, while Georgina was changing the sheeting on one of the beds in the treatment room, Andrew came into the room, searching for some notes, and when they came face to face he, too, appeared rather embarrassed.

'I'm sorry—' Andrew was the first to apologise '—about last night.'

'So am I,' said Georgina quickly. 'I jumped to conclusions. I shouldn't have done. I'm sorry.'

'Shall we just forget it?' Andrew smiled. He looked weary, as if he'd had very little sleep. His dark hair was ruffled, there was shadow on his jaw and his clothes looked a little crumpled, as if they needed ironing.

'Of course.' Georgina nodded, then, struck by his air of dejection and feeling suddenly sorry for him, said, 'Did you really want to take the girls to the pantomime tonight?'

'Well, I would have liked to,' he began, and there was no mistaking the eagerness in his eyes, 'but—'

'You can have my ticket if you like,' Georgina went on quickly. 'I'm sure the girls won't mind.'

'That's not fair,' he replied. 'Tell you what,' he added after a moment, 'I'll ring the theatre and see if they have a spare seat. We may not all be able to sit together but we could perhaps take them for a burger or something afterwards.'

'Well.' Georgina hesitated. That was not what she'd had in mind, but in view of the truce they had effected only moments before it somehow seemed churlish to refuse. 'All right,' she heard herself say.

At that moment an ambulance arrived outside and a patient who had been involved in a road accident was carried into the treatment room on a stretcher. There was no further time for personal discussion as their professional skills were called into play.

'What have we got?' Andrew, who suddenly seemed much more cheerful, turned to Pete Steel.

'This is Mr Neville,' said Pete. 'His car went out of control on a patch of black ice on one of those mini-roundabouts and he collided with a milk float.'

Together with Andrew and Elliot, Pete and, for him, a rather subdued Dave Morey lifted the patient onto the bed.

'Hello, Mr Neville,' Andrew called, then, getting no response from the patient whose eyes were closed, he looked at Pete and said, 'Do we have a first name?'

'Yes,' replied Pete, 'it's Robert.'

'Hello, Robert.' Andrew tried again. 'Can you hear me?'

When there was still no response Georgina, knowing full well Andrew's aversion to abbreviated names, said, 'Why not try Bob?'

Andrew glanced up, his eyes meeting hers, then he bent over the patient again and said, 'Bob? Bob, can you hear me?'

The patient's eyelids flickered and he opened his eyes.

'Right, Staff Nurse Merrick,' said Andrew crisply, 'could we have this patient's clothing removed, please, so that we can do an assessment?'

'Of course, Doctor,' Georgina replied.

They were back to the same rather fragile relationship they had established before the events of the previous night, and Georgina was relieved. She wanted no further friction between them if they were to work amicably together.

Examination revealed that Bob Neville had suffered severe whiplash injuries to his neck, slight concussion and compression of the chest where he had been flung against the steering-wheel. The paramedics had already given him oxygen to assist his breathing, and while Georgina and Helen were fitting a neck brace to immobilise his spine to prevent further injury Andrew, who had been examining the patient's chest, suddenly announced that the man's lung had collapsed.

'You want to do a thoracotomy?' asked Helen.

Andrew nodded. 'Yes, we must relieve the pressure and draw off the fluid.'

Although Georgina had been away from nursing for a long time, she had found herself slipping quite naturally into well-rehearsed routines as different medical procedures presented themselves. Now she automatically assisted Andrew and Helen as—against a backdrop of regular observations to monitor heatbeat, blood pressure and pulse rate—a local anaesthetic, lignocaine, was drawn up and administered, an analgesic, pethidine, was given to ease the pain and an intravenous infusion was set up to restore fluids.

Finally the incision was made and one end of a tubing probe was inserted deeply into the patient's lung to withdraw fluid, which had been rapidly accumulating, while the other end was placed in a container of sterile water.

Gradually Bob Neville's breathing became less laboured, and eventually Andrew gave the word that he could be moved to X-Ray.

After the porters had transferred the patient and the staff were clearing up the treatment area Georgina, suddenly remembering, looked at Andrew. 'Have we any news on Wendy Mills?' she asked.

He nodded. 'Yes, apparently it was an ectopic. She's recovering in Gynae.'

'Poor girl,' said Georgina. 'Will this affect her future chances of conceiving?'

'It could well reduce them,' Andrew replied. 'I went up to see her when she came back from Theatre,' he added.

'How was she?' Suddenly Georgina was curious. It had been a strange case, to say the least.

'It was difficult to say.' Andrew hesitated. 'She was very tearful but that was to be expected. Her mother was with her but there was no sign of the boyfriend—hardly an apt description, I agree,' he added when he caught sight of Georgina's expression, 'but what else would you call him?'

'I know what I'd like to call him,' Georgina said grimly.

'Yes, I can imagine,' Andrew replied.

'So, how was she about losing the baby?'

'Again, difficult to say. Under the circumstances one might have expected relief but I didn't get that impression at all. I felt that not only did she want the baby but that she'd actually planned it.'

'Unbeknown to the slimy Eric, you mean?'

'Well, I can't believe he encouraged it, can you?'

'No, probably not,' Georgina agreed, then sighed. 'But who are we to surmise? Who knows what motives people have or what drives them, come to that? You say her mother came in?'

'Yes, she was with her when I went up. I have to say she seemed to be taking it all in her stride, in spite of Wendy being afraid that she would be shocked.'

'I suspect most mums are pretty unshockable when it really comes down to things,' said Georgina.

At that moment Melanie Jones, the A and E receptionist, looked round the treatment room door. 'Georgina, there's a phone call for you,' she said.

'For me?' Georgina looked up, startled, her first thought being that something had happened to one of the girls. 'Do you know who it is, Melanie?'

'A Dr Phillips, he said,' Melanie replied and, wrinkling her nose, she added, 'I don't think he's one of ours— at least it's an outside line so I wouldn't have thought he was.'

'Oh, no, he isn't,' said Georgina quickly. 'One of ours I mean,' she added, only too aware that Andrew was listening and that Melanie was more than interested.

'Do you want me to put it through in here?' asked Melanie.

'No,' said Georgina quickly, 'I'll come and take it in Reception.' The last thing she wanted was to have to speak to Simon Phillips with Andrew listening, but as she hurried from the treatment room into Reception and picked up the telephone receiver she realised to her dismay that Andrew had followed her. Although he appeared to be deeply engrossed in studying the duty roster Georgina knew only too well that he would hear anything she might say.

'Hello, Simon,' she said.

'Georgina, sorry to ring you at work,' he said. 'Hope it doesn't make a problem for you.'

'Well, I don't think they encourage personal calls on this line,' she said, 'but provided we keep it short. . .'

'Of course. I simply wanted to say sorry for shooting off so quickly last night.'

'That's all right,' she replied. 'I quite understand a doctor's routine.'

'What? Oh, yes, I suppose you would.' He gave a short laugh. 'So, am I forgiven, then?'

'There's really nothing to forgive,' she replied lightly. She was aware that Andrew had lifted his head and appeared to be quite unashamedly listening to what she was saying.

'We'll, that's good,' Simon replied. 'I was wondering if that drink we spoke about could be extended slightly.'

'In what way?'

'Well, I see the Bournemouth Sinfonietta have a concert next Saturday at Sandown, and I wondered if you would like to go.'

Out of the corner of her eye Georgina saw that Denise White had come into Reception from the cubicles where she had been working. She made a beeline for Andrew and began to talk to him, smiling up into his face.

'Georgina?' said Simon. 'Are you still there?'

'Yes,' she said, 'I'm still here, Simon.' She took a deep breath. 'And, yes, I would love to go.' She hadn't meant to say it. Had, in fact, quite made up her mind to refuse if he asked her out, but somehow the sight of Denise smiling up at Andrew in that bewitching way of hers had goaded her into accepting.

'Well, that's marvellous,' Simon replied. 'What about the girls? Will you be able to get a babysitter?'

'Oh, that's not a problem,' she replied airily.

'That's great,' Simon said. 'I'll pick you up around seven.'

'I'll look forward to it, Simon,' she replied. She replaced the receiver and even though Andrew had turned and had his back to her as he laughed and joked with Denise Georgina knew, simply from the set of his head, that he had heard every word.

CHAPTER SEVEN

'WAS it a lovely party, Mummy?' Natasha asked from the back seat of the car.

'Yes, very nice,' Georgina replied. 'Lots of music and chat and lots of people.'

'Was it a disco?' asked Lauren.

'It was. Two of our paramedics organised it and I think they did very well—plenty of old tunes that everyone knew from the sixties and seventies.'

'Yuck,' said Lauren. 'How awful.'

'Did Daddy go?' asked Natasha.

'Yes, he did,' Georgina replied.

'Did he notice you were wearing your red dress?' asked Lauren.

'I think he might have done.' Georgina kept her reply deliberately vague.

Lauren, however, was not to be fobbed off with such an inadequate answer. 'Why do you think that?' she demanded. 'What did he say?'

'Er. . .he said it looked very nice and that he had always liked it.'

'I told you so, didn't I?' There was a triumphant note in Lauren's voice. 'So, when did he say that?'

'What do you mean?' asked Georgina cautiously.

'Well, when did he say it? When did he tell you he'd always liked the dress? Was it when you first arrived?'

'No. . .' Georgina paused on the pretext of negotiating a roundabout, but really deciding how to word her version of events so that her daughters would not go rushing to any false conclusions. It was no good trying to fob them off with half-truths because she knew that Lauren, especi-

102

ally, was more than capable of checking the story with her father when she saw him. 'Actually, it was while we were dancing. . .'

'Dancing!' shrieked Natasha, so loudly that Georgina nearly swerved into the bank.

'Natasha! For goodness' sake! Don't do that!' she cried, gripping the steering-wheel a little more tightly.

'Do what?' said Natasha innocently.

'Shriek like that when I'm driving. You could have caused us to have an accident.'

'Sorry,' mumbled Natasha.

'What were you dancing to?' demanded Lauren.

'What do you mean?' Knowing what was coming next, Georgina desperately played for time.

'What song were you dancing to?' Relentlessly Lauren spelled it out.

'Oh, I don't think I can remember that. . .'

'I know! I know!' Natasha began to bounce up and down in her seat. 'I bet I know. I bet it was ''Lady in Red''. And I bet another thing as well. . .I bet Daddy asked them to play it. Daddy always asked them to play that, didn't he, Laurie? D'you remember when we went to Butlins and then when we were in Spain. . . Daddy always wanted them to play that so he could dance with Mummy.'

Georgina glanced in the driving mirror and her eyes met Lauren's.

'Did he?' asked Lauren.

'He might have done.' Georgina sighed. 'I don't really know. . .you'll have to ask him yourselves.'

'But it may be ages before we see him. . .'

'It's not ages until this evening,' replied Georgina wryly, then waited for the outburst.

'This evening?' It came in chorus. 'Are we seeing him this evening?'

'Yes,' Georgina replied, again glancing in the mirror

and with a pang witnessing for herself the looks of delighted surprise on the girls' faces.

'It was Lauren, ever the practical one, who said, 'But what about the pantomime?'

'Daddy's coming with us. He wanted to come, and we managed to get another ticket. It's in the row behind us but Daddy didn't mind that.'

Lauren, with a deep sigh of contentment, settled back in her seat and said, 'I think that's really neat.'

They were silent for a while after that, obviously digesting what they had been told, and then when they were almost home Lauren said, 'Did you dance with anyone else?'

'Yes.' Georgina nodded.

'Who?' demanded Natasha.

'Well, I danced with Elliot—that's Mr Ferguson, our nursing manager, and I danced with Dr Fleetwood. Oh, yes, and I danced with Dr Phillips. You know Dr Phillips, don't you, Natasha?'

'The man with the golden beard?' squeaked Natasha.

'Yes, that's right. He asked how you were.' Georgina drew up outside their cottage, applied the handbrake and switched off the engine.

'I bet he wasn't as good as Dad,' said Lauren as she scrambled from the back seat.

'As good at what as Dad?' Georgina asked with a laugh as she opened the boot and dragged out the girls' overnight holdall.

'Dancing, of course,' said Lauren. 'Dad's really good at dancing.'

'Yes, he is,' agreed Georgina, locking the car, 'but so is Simon.'

'Is that his name?' Natasha clapped one hand over her mouth and when Georgina nodded she began to chant, '"Simple Simon met a pieman. . .'''

'That's enough, Natasha,' said Georgina firmly, know-

ing how quickly her younger daughter could get out of
control. Moments later, after she'd unlocked the front
door and the two girls had scurried ahead of her up the
stairs, she heard Natasha say, 'I think dancing's soppy,
anyway.'

'I expect Simon was soppy as well,' agreed Lauren.

'Actually,' Natasha replied in the second before their
bedroom door closed and Georgina could hear no more,
'he was very nice and his beard really is just like gold.'

Georgina sighed and went into the kitchen, dumping
her bag onto the floor and standing for a moment and
gazing at her breakfast plate and mug on the draining-
board, together with the two mugs she and Andrew had
used the night before. Best to rinse them and put them
away, she thought, before the girls come down and the
relentless round of questions started again. She couldn't
really imagine what Lauren would make of the fact that
her father had been here in the kitchen after one o'clock
in the morning.

Andrew picked them up in his car to take them to the
theatre, much to the girls' delight. It was the first time
they had been out together as a family since the divorce
and although Georgina was naturally a little apprehensive
about the whole thing even she couldn't help but be
caught up in her daughters' excitement. And she had to
admit that Andrew himself, as he opened the car door
for her and the girls scrambled into the back, seemed
even more boyant than usual. Dressed casually in cords,
sweater and bomber jacket, he looked so like he always
had when they had all lived together that Georgina had
to remind herself firmly that now all that had changed.

The theatre was at Sandown on the far side of the
Island and with every mile the girls' excitement, especially Natasha's, mounted until in the end Georgina had
to remonstrate in an attempt to calm them down.

'I can't help it,' spluttered Natasha. 'I was excited just going to the pantomime but now. . .with Daddy with us as well. . .well! That's really ace!'

'Will you always come with us now?' asked Lauren.

Andrew threw a sidelong glance at Georgina.

'I fear,' she murmured, 'this could be setting a precedent.'

'What's that?' demanded Natasha.

'Oh, for goodness' sake,' said Lauren with a lofty sigh, 'don't you know anything? A president is like a king. America has a president, doesn't it, Dad?'

'Yes,' Andrew agreed with a smile, 'it does.'

'So does that mean Daddy's going to be our president and always come with us when we go anywhere?' asked Natasha.

Andrew risked another glance in Georgina's direction and when she gave a helpless little shake of her head he said, 'Today is a treat for me and for you because it is New Year. Let's just enjoy it and leave it at that, shall we?' When the girls remained silent he went on quickly, 'Now, tell me, I've forgotten, what exactly is this pantomime we're going to see?'

'*Cinderella!*' chorused the girls.

'Good,' said Andrew, 'my favourite. I love the Ugly Sisters.'

'So do I,' said Natasha, then launched into a lengthy account of exactly why she liked them.

Georgina stared out of the car window and mentally switched off from the girls' chatter and Andrew's amused replies. It was almost dark and the weather was turning much colder, the outlines of the bare trees lining the road starkly silhouetted against the lighter sky. It was warm and comfortable in Andrew's car and for the moment Georgina was content to relax and let him take control.

If she was honest she was feeling very tired as the past week finally caught up with her. Her return to work had taken quite a bit of getting used to, fitting in her shifts with the needs of the girls and the many other demands of running a home. With all that coming, as it had, hot on the heels of Christmas and the New Year celebrations, she was feeling quite exhausted.

Her emotions also had taken something of a battering for over and above the usual highly emotional seasons she'd had to contend not only with working alongside Andrew but also with his current girlfriend. And, if all that hadn't been enough, she'd been asked out for the first time since her divorce.

Even her relationship with Andrew seemed to have changed in some way in the last few days. She was uncertain in what way exactly it had changed, found it difficult to put her finger on really, for she had prided herself that they had established a civilised relationship since they had finally parted which was beneficial to the girls. Somehow the balance of that seemed to have shifted slightly but whether it was because they now worked together or not, she didn't really know.

The night before had bothered her although she was loath to admit it, even to herself. Dancing with Andrew and being close to him again had stirred all sorts of feelings and emotions that were really better left alone, and then having to contend with his possible jealousy over Simon had left her feeling confused. The kiss, she knew, should never have happened. That sort of thing did neither of them any good, dwelling on what might have been instead of positively concentrating on what was.

She glanced at him again, at the familiar profile visible in the half-light. And now here they were going out together as a family, suggested by her in a moment of weakness—a moment she feared she might very much live to regret if the girls' reactions were anything to go by.

The pantomime came up to everyone's expectations

and Georgina found even her troubled mood of earlier
was swept away as she joined in with the rest of the
audience in their conspiracy with Buttons against the
Ugly Sisters.

Andrew's seat was directly behind her own, and as
the evening progressed Georgina found she was intensely
aware of his presence. Whereas at one time she might
have found that irritating now, to her surprise, she found
it not only comforting but strangely stimulating.

In the interval he leaned forward and, resting his chin
on her shoulder, said, 'Can I buy you an ice cream?'

It was what he'd said that very first time all those
years ago when he'd met her from the café and walked
along the Esplanade with her. They'd often joked about
it since and now he'd said it again because he knew she
would remember. Turning her head slightly, she found
his face literally an inch or two away from her own.

'That would be nice,' she said lightly, 'but I mustn't
miss my bus.'

Andrew chuckled and stood up while Natasha turned
to Georgina and said solemnly, 'We don't have to go
home on the bus, do we?'

'No, darling, we don't,' replied Georgina.

'But, you said. . .'

'It was a joke,' explained Georgina, 'a joke between
Daddy and Mummy, that's all.'

'But. . .' Natasha would have persisted but Lauren
silenced her.

'Shut up,' she said. 'It's private, nothing to do
with you.'

That seemed to suffice and Natasha fell silent, remain-
ing so even after Andrew returned with tubs of ice cream,
the lights dimmed and the curtain rose again.

Later, on the way home, he stopped in Newport and
took them all to McDonald's where they sat on high
stools and ate cheese burgers and fries and the girls drank

Coke while Andrew and herself drank tea from huge cardboard cups.

'That was wonderful!' Blissfully Natasha wiped tomato sauce from her mouth with the back of her hand, earning a reproachful look from Georgina who handed her a paper serviette. 'Will you come indoors, Daddy, when we get home? I want to show you my book I had for Christmas from Granny.'

'Well,' said Andrew, 'I guess that's up to Mummy.' Glancing at Georgina, he raised his eyebrows and both girls turned expectantly to her.

'How can I refuse?' she said.

And somehow, when they finally reached the cottage, it seemed the most natural thing in the world after the evening they had just had for him to come inside.

Natasha showed him her book and Lauren discussed with him the project she was doing at school. At last Andrew glanced at his watch. 'I'd better be going,' he said.

'Oh, no, not yet,' wailed Natasha.

'I don't want to outstay my welcome.' Andrew allowed his gaze to meet Georgina's, and she was forced to look away.

'You'll see Daddy again at the weekend,' she said. Hesitating slightly, she went on, 'Actually, Andrew, I was wondering whether the girls could stay with you on Saturday night. I have...I have the chance to go to a recital by the Bournemouth Sinfonietta...'

'That could be a bit of a problem,' he said.

'Oh...?'

'Yes, you see, I've started decorating my spare room...'

'Oh, well, never mind...'

'But, not to worry, I could come here until you get back, if you like.'

'Well.' She hesitated, her mind leaping ahead to what

could be the embarrassing scenario of Simon bringing her home to find her ex-husband babysitting.

'Oh, yes.' It was Lauren who took the matter out of her hands. 'I'll have finished the next part of my project by then, Dad, and you could check it with me. We won't have time in the afternoon, will we, if we go to the ice rink?'

'That's true,' Andrew agreed calmly. 'So that's settled, then. I'll come here and look after the girls while you go to your concert.'

A few minutes later, as the girls waved Andrew off, Georgina had the feeling that somehow he had deduced from the telephone conversation he'd overheard that it was Simon she was going out with, and consequently had contrived the whole thing by saying he was decorating the bedroom the girls used at his flat just so that he would be in the cottage when she returned.

'I didn't know you were going to a concert,' said Lauren a moment later as she closed the front door and came back into the sitting-room.

'Who are you going with?' demanded Natasha.

Georgina took a deep breath. 'Dr Phillips, actually,' she said.

'Not Simple Simon?' giggled Natasha.

'Natasha, you are not to call him that!' said Georgina crossly.

'Why? Is he your boyfriend?' Natasha was still giggling but Georgina noticed that Lauren was frowning.

'What's the matter Lauren?' she said, and it came out a little more sharply than she had intended. 'Why are you looking like that?'

'Does Dad know about this?' asked Lauren primly. 'About who you're going with, I mean.'

'Why?' said Georgina. 'Should that make a difference?'

'I think he might want to know,' Lauren replied in the same prim tones.

'So are you saying it's OK for Dad to have a girlfriend but not for me to have a boyfriend? Is that it?' asked Georgina.

Lauren didn't answer, just kicked the edge of the rug with the toe of her trainers, and Georgina said, 'Anyway, Simon—Dr Phillips—isn't my boyfriend, as it happens. He is just a very nice man who has offered to take me to a concert, that's all.'

'Actually,' said Lauren quietly, 'I don't think it's OK for Dad to have a girlfriend, any more than it would be for you to have a boyfriend.'

'Lauren,' said Georgina gently, 'you have to understand that Dad and I are divorced now. We've both been on our own for some time and it's pretty inevitable that we shall have other friends. . .'

'Like Denise,' Natasha chipped in solemnly.

'Yes. . .' Georgina hesitated. 'Like Denise. . .'

The matter was left there but the whole thing somehow made Georgina feel very uneasy. It had taken a long time for her to even think of going out with anyone else, and now that she had agreed to it she could well do without the disapproval of her daughters and the interference of her ex-husband.

The weather grew even colder during the rest of that first week of the new year, with snow flurries, icy patches on the roads and early morning freezing fog. These conditions all contributed to the inevitable spate of accidents which kept the A and E staff busy.

On one particular morning Georgina found herself working with Denise White in the nurses' station and with the walking wounded who had been allocated to cubicles to await treatment. She had not seen very much of Denise since her arrival at the Shalbrooke as their shifts had not really coincided or, if they had, one had been in the treatment rooms and the other on cubicles.

Georgina had not been sorry for this as she doubted that she and Andrew's current girlfriend could have much to say to each other. In a way she wished the situation could have been different because in spite of everything she liked the girl. She was pleasant, attractive and had a very good sense of humour which, when Georgina thought about it, wasn't really surprising, knowing Andrew and his preferences as she did. The girl was also a good nurse and as they worked she spoke of her future plans.

'I would like to go into midwifery,' she said in a brief lull between patients.

'That used to be my plan until I started having babies of my own,' replied Georgina, 'then somehow, I don't know, that all seemed to go by the board.'

'I would like a family one day,' Denny replied. 'Not just yet. . .' She paused and Georgina found herself wondering what was coming next and just how much this girl knew about her and her situation. 'On the other hand, I was only saying the other day that I wouldn't want to leave it too long,' she added. 'Your girls are lovely,' she went on. 'So many kids these days are pretty awful—you know, downright precocious—but Lauren and Natasha aren't like that at all—must be something to do with their upbringing. I can't imagine you or Andrew standing any nonsense.'

'I dare say Andrew is softer with them than I am,' said Georgina.

'But he can afford to be. . .it's you who has to live with them and have all the day-to-day discipline to enforce.'

'Quite,' agreed Georgina faintly, thinking how bizarre this conversation was becoming. She hadn't realised that the relationship between Andrew and this girl had gone so far but at the same time she found herself wondering what Andrew's reaction had been on learning that Denise was so keen to have a family in the not too distant future.

She couldn't imagine Andrew with other children, children who weren't anything to do with her. Neither could she imagine Lauren and Natasha with this young girl as their stepmother, perhaps living with her some-times—calling her Mummy.

She gave herself a little shake in an attempt to banish the disturbing images from her mind, then was forced to concentrate as another patient arrived, accompanied by two paramedics and Norman Westfield, the A and E porter.

'This is Emily—Mrs Sanderson,' said Norman cheer-fully. 'She slipped on the ice. Didn't you, love?' He looked down at the patient, a well-dressed woman in her seventies who was quite obviously in a great deal of pain.

'Hello, Emily,' said Georgina. 'Let's get you onto a trolley and make you comfortable. Then we'll take some details, and get a doctor to come and examine you.' While Denny was helping Norman and one of the paramedics to transfer Mrs Sanderson onto a care trolley and wheel her into a cubicle Georgina turned to the second paramedic. 'What do we know?' she asked.

'She fell heavily,' he said. 'She tried to get up, appar-ently, but couldn't put any weight on her left leg.'

'Any sign of other injury?'

'Don't think so. . .but. . .' The man paused.

'Yes, what?' asked Georgina, knowing that any detail, however small, could help with the patient's treatment.

'Well, I don't suppose it's anything much, but in the ambulance she kept on about someone called Tommy. . . In fact, she seemed more concerned about Tommy than she did about her leg. . . Couldn't get it out of her exactly who Tommy is, though. . .'

'Her husband?' asked Georgina, lowering her voice so that the patient wouldn't hear.

'I don't think so somehow. . .' The man hesitated again then shook his head. 'No, I didn't get that impression. She spoke almost as if he was a child.'

'A grandchild, possibly?'

'Maybe,' the paramedic replied, but he sounded far from sure.

'All right,' said Georgina, 'leave it to us. We'll see what we can find out. Whoever he is, if she's that worried about him we'll need to know.'

Between them Georgina and Denny carefully examined Emily Sanderson for any further injuries, then carried out routine observations of pulse rate and blood pressure to assess her general cardiovascular state. These readings were within acceptable levels, which suggested she had not sustained any internal injuries or bleeding.

'Now, Emily,' said Georgina as Denny entered the readings onto a patient chart, 'we're going to undress you and slip on a hospital gown.'

Until that moment Emily Sanderson had been lying quietly, mostly with her eyes closed. Now her eyes snapped open and she glared at Georgina.

'I haven't got time for that,' she said. 'I have to get home.'

'We can't let you go home yet—you need to have X-rays first,' explained Georgina.

'And then what?' demanded Emily, her gaze darting suspiciously from Georgina to Denny then back again.

'Well, it depends on what the X-ray shows up. Your leg may just be badly bruised or, on the other hand you may have cracked the bone, in which case you may need to go to Theatre. . .'

'I can't possibly mess about like that,' said Emily. 'I must get home—Tommy will be wondering where I've got to. I've left him on his own, you see.'

'Is Tommy your husband, Emily?' asked Georgina,

and succeeded in earning herself a withering look from Emily.

'Would you like us to phone for you—to explain to Tommy what has happened?' Denny tried a different tack and when Emily shook her head she went on, 'Alternatively, we could bring the phone trolley in here and you could phone Tommy yourself.'

'I couldn't do that.' Emily looked irritated, as if the whole idea was totally out of the question and as if Denny should have known better than to even suggest it. 'He'll be worried to death,' she muttered, half to herself.

Georgina looked at Denny and raised her eyebrows but the girl helplessly shook her head. Turning back to Emily, Georgina said, 'In that case, Emily, is there someone else we could phone—someone who could perhaps go to your house and tell Tommy what has happened?'

'Now that really would upset him,' snapped Emily. 'He doesn't like strangers.'

'Well, what about a neighbour or a relative?'

Emily shook her head. 'There's no one else now.'

'Emily—' Georgina tried again '—who exactly is Tommy?'

But Emily's mouth had settled into a stubborn thin line and in the end all the two staff nurses could do was to persuade her to let them remove her tweed suit and her twin set and help her into a white hospital gown. It was quite obvious she was in great deal of pain and they endeavoured to be as gentle as possible.

'I'm sorry about the pain,' Georgina said as she slipped a pillow beneath Emily's leg to support it, 'but that should help to make you a little more comfortable.'

'Can't you give me an aspirin or something?' she muttered as Georgina began folding her clothes.

'I'm sorry, we can't,' Georgina replied, 'not until you've seen the doctor and we know whether or not you need to have an anaesthetic.'

'Call yourself nurses!' Emily snorted.

At that moment the curtain was whisked aside and Andrew came into the cubicle. His expression softened when he saw who was on duty, but whether it was from finding herself there or Denny, Georgina didn't know. Pushing the thought to the back of her mind, she outlined Emily Sanderson's history to Andrew, and while he was examining the patient she and Denny stood back.

'Who do you think Tommy is?' murmured Denny out of the side of her mouth.

'Goodness knows,' Georgina whispered back.

'I reckon it's her cat,' said Denny.

'Could well be. In my experience, people worry far more about their animals than they do about humans,' said Georgina with a wry smile.

At last Andrew straightened up and turned from the patient. 'We need to get Mrs Sanderson to X-Ray,' he said. 'That's a nasty crack to her hip she's had there. I think we could be talking about a fractured neck of femur but we won't know for sure until after the X-ray. Now, do we have any other problems?' he asked, taking the chart from Denny and studying it.

'Only Tommy,' replied Georgina solemnly. 'Mrs Sanderson is very worried about Tommy because she's left him on his own.'

'Do we know exactly who Tommy is?' asked Andrew.

They all looked at Emily but she had leaned her head back against the pillows again and closed her eyes.

'Not really,' Denny replied, 'although we did wonder. . .' Raising her voice slightly, she said, 'Is Tommy your cat, Emily?'

'Cat!' Emily's eyes flew open again and she glared at them all. 'How dare you call Tommy a cat!'

'So will you tell us now who Tommy is?' asked Georgina.

Emily gave a deep sigh then, looking directly at

Andrew, said, 'I'd like to speak to you, young man. On your own,' she added darkly.

'Very well.' Andrew glanced at the two nurses and said, 'Maybe you could arrange for a porter to take Mrs Sanderson to X-Ray while we are talking.'

They nodded, moved out of the cubicle and Georgina drew the curtain behind her.

'She didn't like that,' Denny chuckled. 'Us thinking Tommy was a cat. He's probably a dog after all that.'

'Or maybe a parrot.' Georgina smiled. 'Anyway, what ever he is she wasn't prepared to tell a mere nurse. Obviously only a doctor would do.'

While Denny telephoned the X-ray unit Georgina went to find Norman.

'Is she ready to go down now?' asked the porter, whom she eventually found talking to Dot in the nurses' station.

'Not quite,' Georgina replied. 'Andrew is still with her—oh, here he comes now,' she added as Andrew appeared in the passage that led into Reception from the cubicles.

Denny turned from the phone and as Andrew approached she said, 'So what is he, then, the mysterious Tommy? A goldfish. . .or a pet tarantula, maybe?' She was laughing as she said it but to Georgina, who knew Andrew so well, just one look at his face told her that what he had heard from Emily Sanderson, far from being amusing, was, in fact, very serious indeed.

CHAPTER EIGHT

'I PERSUADED her to allow me to alert the necessary authorities.' Andrew glanced round at the others who were assembled in the nurses' station for a case conference on Emily Sanderson.

'So how old did you say Tommy is?' asked Denny incredulously.

'Nearly forty, apparently,' replied Andrew.

'Hang on a minute,' said Elliot. 'Can we get this straight? Tommy is Emily Sanderson's son, is that right?'

'Yes.' Andrew nodded. 'He suffers from Down's syndrome and apparently Emily has cared for him on her own since the death of her husband five years ago. Her husband was a professor of genealogy at a university in the north, and on his retirement seven years ago they moved to the Island.'

'So why wouldn't she tell us who Tommy was?' asked Georgina.

'That's the amazing part,' said Andrew. 'Apparently, no one knows about Tommy. At least no one here on the Island, that is. He never goes out these days and it seems not even their neighbours know of his existence.'

'But that's terrible.' Denny looked aghast. 'How could she be so cruel as to keep him locked away like that?'

'I doubt whether Emily sees it that way,' said Andrew. 'Remember, Tommy would have been born in a very different climate from that of today, and his mother probably sincerely believes she is protecting him from a terrifying world.'

'She could be right,' observed Elliot dryly.

'So what's happening now?' asked Helen Turner,

who had remained silent until that moment.

'Emily's X-rays have revealed a nasty fracture to the neck of the left femur, which is what I suspected,' said Andrew. 'She'll have to go to Theatre. She eventually, though reluctantly, agreed for me to contact the police and Social Services to go to her house in Gurnard and to talk to Tommy and arrange care for him.'

'What do you think they'll do?' asked Georgina anxiously.

'I don't know.' Andrew shrugged. 'I suspect some sort of residential care will be necessary. I think Emily had guessed that, but didn't want to admit it. . .' He paused as Melanie suddenly appeared and told him that Social Services were on the phone for him.

'If you'll excuse me, I'll go and see what they've arranged.' Andrew nodded at the rest of the staff, then disappeared into the office.

'God, I feel awful now,' said Denny. 'Fancy thinking Tommy was her cat. Whatever must she have thought of me?'

'You weren't to know,' said Helen, 'and, besides, plenty of patients are anxious about their pets.'

'I know. . .but there's a vast difference between a cat and a handicapped son of forty!'

'Poor Emily,' said Georgina. 'I feel so sorry for her. Fancy struggling to care for him all these years on her own. She must have felt very isolated.'

'I know the feeling, believe me,' said Helen quietly.

'You mean, with your father?' Georgina threw her a quick look.

Helen nodded. 'Yes, I feel isolated sometimes. . . locked in a world with just him and me, with no one else really understanding, and, heaven only knows, I have help and back-up. Goodness knows how poor Emily Sanderson manages, coping entirely on her own.'

'Surely she could have had help if she'd asked for

it?' said Denny. 'After all, this isn't exactly the Dark Ages, is it?'

'I think you'll find it's like Andrew said,' replied Helen. 'We live in a much more enlightened society today where conditions like Down's syndrome are concerned.

'Forty years ago it was a very different matter. All I can say is thank goodness attitudes have changed. I only wish that change could extend a little more to include a greater understanding of Alzheimer's disease. I get so angry when people treat my father like some sort of half-wit when I know what an intelligent and articulate man he once was. It must be the same for Emily. Only she knows Tommy's capabilities. And she has obviously chosen not to subject him to possible ridicule and ignorance.'

'Lets hope it's that and not that she's ashamed of him,' said Elliot.

'As a mother myself, I prefer to go along with Helen's theory,' said Georgina, glancing up as Andrew returned.

'It makes you wonder, doesn't it?' said Denny suddenly, and everyone, including Andrew, looked at her. 'They say a parent never stops worrying about a child— I'm beginning to think that must be right.'

Briefly Andrew's gaze met Georgina's and as he glanced round at the others an expectant hush fell.

'The police and Social Services have contacted Tommy,' he said. 'He was understandably very distressed and a social worker is bringing him into the hospital to see his mother.' He paused. 'Georgina,' he said, turning to look at her again, 'when they come in I will take them to see Emily. I would like you to come as well.'

'Of course,' she murmured, and quite suddenly for some unknown reason she felt a rush of warmth that Andrew had chosen her. He could quite easily have asked Denny or even Helen but he hadn't—he'd chosen her.

Almost immediately she tried to dismiss the thought. This was no time to be getting sentimental.

Tommy Sanderson arrived half an hour later in the company of a social worker. Andrew and Georgina met him in Reception. He was dressed in grey flannel trousers, a white, open-necked shirt and a camel duffle-coat. He looked frightened and bewildered and held tightly to the social worker's hand. In his other hand he clutched a comic.

'Hello, Tommy.' Andrew held out his hand but Tommy shied away and hid his face.

'You try,' Andrew murmured softly to Georgina. 'I think he may respond better to a woman.'

'Tommy.' Georgina succeeded in taking his hand as the social worker released it. 'Shall we go and see your mum? She's hurt her leg and she's not able to walk at the moment, but I know she wants to see you.'

Watching him closely, Georgina knew she'd got his attention as a tiny frown creased his smooth forehead and blinking rapidly, he said, 'Mam?'

'That's right,' Georgina said as together they began to walk down the passage. 'She's waiting to see you now. I say, Tommy, is that the *Beano* you have there? I like the *Beano*. I like Dennis the Menace, don't you?'

Tommy nodded and looked up at Georgina, giving her a quite radiant smile as she gently led him into the cubicle where Emily Sanderson lay on the trolley, waiting to go to Theatre.

'Tommy.' Emily held out her hand when she saw her son, while Tommy stopped dead and stared at her. Then his face puckered as if he was about to cry. 'Come here, Tommy,' Emily went on, and at last Tommy moved to the side of the bed and, leaning over, rested his head against his mother's body. Gently Emily began to stroke his short, fluffy hair. 'I want you to be a very good boy,' she said. 'I have to stay here for a while. . .'

'Bad leg. . .' said Tommy.

'Yes, I have a bad leg.' Emily nodded. 'Someone will look after you, Tommy, a nice lady. You must be a very good boy, do as she tells you and eat up all your food. I will be home again soon.'

Tommy snuffled into the white cellular blanket that covered his mother's knees. Lifting his head, he looked at Georgina. 'Nice lady,' he said.

Further explanation had to follow that it wasn't Georgina who was to look after him but for the moment Tommy was content, and after spending a happy ten minutes or so with Emily he was taken back to the car by the social worker.

He waved to Georgina from the back window of the car and as he was driven away she turned to Andrew, finding her eyes quite damp. 'Where is he going?' she asked.

'Social Services have arranged for him to go into their residential centre until Emily has recovered,' Andrew replied.

'It could open up a whole new world for him,' she said as Andrew held the door open for her and they went back into A and E Reception. 'He may not even want to go home.'

'Oh, I don't know.' Andrew grinned. 'There's no one like your mum, is there?'

'True,' Georgina agreed, 'but Emily won't be around for ever, and caring for Tommy must be getting increasingly difficult for her as it is.'

'Well, who knows what will happen? We'll just have to wait and see. Anyway, for the time being, Emily will go to Theatre and have her femur set. . .' Andrew paused and looked down at her. 'Thanks for your help with Tommy,' he added softly. 'I knew you would be the right one to handle the situation.'

'Thanks.' Again she felt a warm glow inside, then the

moment passed as Helen called her from her office and Andrew took himself off to the treatment room where another patient awaited his attention.

When Georgina entered the sister's office Helen was standing behind her desk, fiddling with some pens. She looked up and smiled when she saw Georgina. 'Shut the door,' she said, 'and come and take a seat.'

'Goodness!' said Georgina. 'That sounds ominous. Is there something wrong?'

'Not at all,' Helen replied. 'I simply wanted a bit of a chat, that's all, and to give you this.' She leaned over the desk and picked up a blue folder which she handed to Georgina, before sitting down herself.

'What is it?' Georgina frowned. The cover of the folder was blank.

'It's your schedule for your refresher course—lectures, classes, that sort of thing,' said Helen.

'Oh, I see.' Georgina felt a momentary stab of relief. She had wondered what this was all about, fearing perhaps that her work was giving cause for concern.

'You'll see,' Helen went on after a moment, 'that your lectures start next week. The first is by Richard Fleetwood and is on anaesthetics—that will be here in the hospital teaching centre.'

'Do you think I'll have much home study?' asked Georgina, opening the folder and flipping through the loose leaves that gave the details of her course.

'There will be a bit,' Helen admitted. She paused. 'Will that pose a problem?'

'No. No, of course not,' Georgina replied quickly. 'It's only the time element, that's all. I shall probably enjoy the study itself. I loved the theory side of things when I was training.'

'It makes a change to hear that,' said Helen. 'Most girls only want to be on the wards.' She paused, her eyes narrowing slightly as she looked at Georgina across the desk. 'You're not finding it too much, are you? Working again and looking after the girls?'

'No, not at all,' said Georgina. 'Oh, I dare say I could do with a few more hours in each day but I suspect that's the same for all working mums. And, yes, before you ask, I am feeling tired, but I guess it's early days yet and there's bound to be a certain amount of adjustment. . .'

Helen nodded. 'That's inevitable, I suppose.' She hesitated and picked up one of the pens she'd been toying with, rolling it between her fingers. 'And how's it working out, you being here with Andrew?' she said at last.

'It's OK,' Georgina said. 'In actual fact, it's much better than I had feared and that's probably because we've all moved on.'

'How do you mean, moved on?' Helen looked up and frowned.

'New relationships, that sort of thing,' said Georgina bright—almost flippantly, she hoped—as if to convince Helen, and probably herself as well, that any new relationships really weren't of too much consequence.

'New relationships?' said Helen slowly.

'Yes.' Georgina laughed. 'I have a date. . .how about that?'

'A date? Who with?' Helen stared at her.

'Simon Phillips. He's asked me to go to the Bournemouth Sinfonietta concert with him.'

'Is that a fact?' said Helen softly. She paused. 'So, is he the first? Since Andrew, I mean.'

'Oh, yes.' Georgina gave a short, forced laugh. 'Yes, he's the first. Very much so. So much so, in fact, that I think I shall have to brush up on my dating techniques. I gather things are very different these days. . . Having said that, Andrew doesn't seem to have had any bother in that direction so I don't see why I should!'

'That was all over for Andrew a long time ago,' said Helen quietly. 'In fact, and I guess I'm sticking my neck out here, I would go so far as to say that he probably feels now that it was some sort of nightmare that happened in another life. . .'

'Couldn't have been that much of a nightmare for him to want to repeat the experience,' retorted Georgina as quick as a flash.

'What do you mean, repeat the experience?' Helen stared at her across the desk.

'What I say,' replied Georgina lightly. 'After all, he hasn't exactly wasted a lot of time, has he? I must admit I was a bit surprised when I found out that she worked here. I wish I'd known that beforehand.' She gave a tight little smile. 'I'm not sure it would have made any difference to my decision to apply for the job but to be forewarned is to be forearmed and it would have been nice to be prepared. Oh, I knew he had a girlfriend,' she went on quickly, giving Helen no chance to intervene. 'Natasha had already told me that—what I didn't know was where she worked. . .' She trailed off as she realised that Helen was staring at her in open astonishment. 'What is it?' she asked. 'Why are you looking at me like that?'

'I don't know what you're talking about,' said Helen faintly. 'I didn't have the slightest idea that Andrew had a girlfriend, let alone that it was someone who worked here.'

Georgina frowned. 'I gathered it was common know-ledge,' she said. 'At least, Denise seems quite open about it.'

'Denise?' Helen looked more baffled than ever. 'You mean Denny—our Denny?'

Georgina nodded. 'Yes.'

'I think you must be mistaken,' said Helen, slowly putting her pen down but still staring at Georgina in amazement.

'Oh, I don't think so.' Georgina attempted flippancy again. 'The girls have seen her at Andrew's flat, and she's even been out with them on occasion. And Denise herself has told me she's hoping to marry soon. . .even talks of starting a family.'

'Yes, but not with Andrew.' Helen shook her head in disbelief.

'Is that so hard to believe?' Georgina gave a short laugh. 'Younger women are often attracted to older men, you know, and, let's face it, there's not that much of an age difference between them. . .'

'No,' Helen interrupted her, 'I wasn't meaning that. . .'

'Then what?'

'Simply that I knew Denny had a boyfriend, but I understood it to be someone else. . .a young man who works for a solicitor in Ryde, to be exact. The last I heard, it was him she was planning to marry.'

'Well, things have obviously changed since then.' Abruptly Georgina stood up. 'I'd better get back,' she said. 'There were a lot of people in Reception when I came in.' She turned to the door but Helen stopped her.

'Georgie,' she said, and there was a wealth of concern in her voice.

'Yes?' Georgina answered, without turning.

'Georgie, if this is true about Andrew and Denny then I owe you an apology.'

'Why?' she asked lightly, her back still to Helen.

'Well, if I had known they were having a relationship I would never have asked you to come here to work. Never in a million years would I have asked you.'

Georgina swallowed then, taking a deep breath and from somewhere summoning a smile, she turned at last to face Helen. 'I can't think why,' she said. 'After all, as I keep reminding people, Andrew and I are divorced now and what either of us does, or with whom, can be of no possible interest to the other.'

Helen watched Georgina go in dismay, hardly able to believe what she had just heard and that she could have been so wrong over her interpretation of the relationships amongst her staff. She'd watched both Andrew and Georgina closely in the days since the party and she could have sworn she'd seen something between them—nothing tangible, more a growing awareness of each other once more, but enough to have made her feel that her wish of a reconciliation between these two people of whom she was so fond might be more than just a possibility.

But now this revelation from Georgina that Andrew was having an affair with Denny White seemed to put paid to all her fond theories. Helen sat down at her desk and began to fiddle with her pen.

Could Georgina be mistaken? Helen had certainly been under the impression that Denny was still involved with her young solicitor. But Georgina had implied that the affair between Denny and Andrew was pretty advanced, even to the stage where they were thinking of making it permanent and talking of marriage. So had Denny been two-timing her young man?

Helen frowned and shook her head. She didn't seem to be able to keep up with people these days. They seemed to shed relationships and enter new ones at the drop of a hat. Maybe she was getting old, she thought ruefully, but, whatever, she was disappointed, she had to admit that. She had really thought something had been about to happen between the Merricks again. It would have been lovely and so nice for those girls, who quite obviously wanted nothing more than to see their parents back together again. The telephone on her desk suddenly rang, breaking into her thoughts. Helen sighed and wearily reached out her hand to answer it.

Georgina tried hard to look forward to her date with Simon Phillips, but as the day drew near she found she was filled more with apprehension than anything else.

The day itself fell on the Saturday of her free weekend, a day she spent catching up on household chores and shopping while the girls were out with Andrew. The arrangement was that he would take them out for something to eat then would return to the cottage where he would stay with them while Georgina went out with Simon.

By the time she had finished the chores, showered and changed into a long ribbed skirt and a matching sweater in soft wool and had arranged her hair into an attractive plait she was feeling quite sick with nerves. Whether this was from the thought of the date itself or from Andrew's involvement in the proceedings, she wasn't quite sure. She only knew that when Andrew arrived on the doorstep with the girls her nerves felt as if they were ready to snap.

'It's snowing!' breathed Natasha ecstatically.

'Is it?' Georgina looked anxiously beyond the little group on the step.

'It's not very much,' said Andrew, his gaze wandering over her and taking in every inch of her appearance.

'But it's lying!' Lauren sounded every bit as excited as Natasha and as they moved forward into the light from the hall lamp Georgina could see the snowflakes sticking to their eyelashes and nestling between Natasha's dark curls.

'Perhaps there'll be enough for a snowman this time,' said Lauren as Andrew closed the door behind him and they all struggled out of their coats, scarves and gloves.

'Have you had your tea?' asked Georgina as Natasha bounded into the sitting-room and switched on the television.

Lauren nodded. 'Yes, we had fish fingers, chips and beans.'

'In a café?'

'No, at Daddy's,' she replied. Then, screwing up her

eyes and peering at Georgina, she said, 'You've done your hair differently.'

'Have I?' She answered casually but was aware out of the corner of her eye that Andrew was watching her. 'I used to wear it like this for work—a long time ago.'

'I don't remember it,' said Lauren.

'I do,' said Andrew softly. 'It suits you.'

'Yes, well.' She tried to appear brisk and efficient as she supervised the girls but, realising her cheeks had grown warm under Andrew's scrutiny, knew she was failing miserably.

'What time are you going out?' Lauren called from halfway up the stairs.

Georgina glanced at her watch, the one Andrew had bought her on their fifth wedding anniversary. 'In about ten minutes' time,' she replied.

'We had a brilliant day,' called Natasha from the sitting-room where she was sitting on the carpet in front of the television, 'didn't we, Daddy?'

'We certainly did.' Andrew strolled into the room and sat down in an armchair, the chair they had brought with them from the other house—the chair he had always sat in when they had all been together. He looked so right, so natural, that Georgina, still on edge from the incongruity of the situation, was forced to look away. 'Your skating is really coming on, isn't it, poppet? I think we could have the next Jayne Torvill here,' he said with a grin.

'So, have you changed your mind about working in a fish shop?' Georgina smiled down at her younger daughter.

'Yes,' Natasha replied, without looking round. 'Denise says if I practise really hard I could be a 'fessional ice skater.'

'Did Denise go with you today?' asked Georgina casually.

'Mmm.' Natasha nodded. 'She cooked our fish fingers as well, didn't she, Daddy?'

Andrew had picked up a newspaper and was scanning the sports pages, and his reply was little more than a vague nod.

At that moment there came the sound of a car outside and Georgina drew back the curtain and looked out. 'Here's my. . .' She hesitated, not knowing quite how to describe Simon. She could hardly say, 'my date.' 'Here's my lift,' she said feebly at last, aware that Andrew had lowered his newspaper and was watching her again. 'I must go. . . Don't let the girls stay up too late, Andrew. Natasha in bed by half past eight and Lauren by nine.'

'That's not fair!' wailed Natasha.

'It's perfectly fair.' Georgina dropped a kiss on the top of her small daughter's head. 'I'll see you later, Andrew,' she said, without looking at him, totally unable to face the expression in his eyes. 'I. . .I shouldn't be too late.' Hurrying into the hall, she called up the stairs, 'Night, Lauren, God bless.' Then her voice trailed off as Lauren suddenly appeared at the top of the stairs, an accusing expression on her sullen little face.

She fled, grabbing her coat and struggling into it as she went, out of the cottage and down the path—almost slipping on the light covering of snow in her haste to get to Simon's car waiting at the gate.

He got out of the car and opened the door for her, his golden beard and hair gleaming in the streetlight. While she was fastening her seat belt he got back into the car and, glancing back at the lighted windows of the cottage, said, 'You managed to find a babysitter, then?'

She nodded, carefully keeping her gaze straight ahead and willing herself not to look at the cottage, afraid that if she did so she would see Andrew or the girls looking out of the window.

'Your mother?' he asked as they drove away.

'No,' Georgina shook her head, 'not my mother. My. . .the girls' father, actually.'

'Oh. . .oh, I see,' Simon replied.

The evening was not a disaster but neither, on the other hand, was it a great success. The concert was everything it should have been, the programme varied and the music a delight. Simon was attentive and charming, if a little serious at times, but for some perverse reason all Georgina could think about was that Andrew was at home in the cottage with the girls.

At one point she even found herself wondering if she wouldn't rather be there with them in front of the fire, possibly playing Scrabble, instead of sitting beside Simon Phillips, a man—nice as he was—she scarcely knew, in an overheated theatre on a cold January night. Which was ridiculous, really, she told herself sternly as the interval approached, especially when she had been eager to go out—to start to make a new life for herself.

During the interval, over a drink in the bar, in a desperate attempt to draw the conversation away from her and at her prompting, Simon told her a little about himself. In some ways their situations seemed similar for while Simon hadn't been married he'd had a long-term relationship which had recently ended.

'You could say, I suppose, this locum job is therapy while I lick my wounds,' he said ruefully.

'You're still in love with her?' asked Georgina, suddenly interested.

He shrugged. 'Let's just say I didn't want the break up. Nearly four years is a long time to live with someone.'

'It must have been like being married,' said Georgina thoughtfully.

'Yes. . .' Simon hesitated. 'Yes, I suppose it was. Still, life goes on. . .or so everyone tells me, so there's no point looking back.'

Inevitably the conversation turned to herself—to her own situation and to Andrew.

'Would you ever take him back?' asked Simon, draining his glass as the second bell sounded.

'I don't think I could trust him again,' said Georgina.

'Ah,' Simon replied.

It was snowing heavily when they left the theatre, making the roads slippery and dangerous.

'Let's hope they get the gritting lorries out soon,' said Simon as he drove slowly back through the country lanes to Newtown, 'otherwise it will be chaos in the morning. Are you on an early shift?'

'No,' Georgina replied, peering ahead through the windsceen at the swirling snowflakes. 'Luckily, I have another day off tomorrow. How about you?'

'No such luck—I'm on call,' Simon replied, swearing under his breath as the car skidded slightly as they approached a deserted crossroads.

It was well past eleven o'clock when they reached the cottage, and as Simon switched off the engine Georgina threw him an apprehensive glance. 'Would you like to come inside for coffee?' she asked.

'If you don't mind,' he said, 'I think, in view of this weather, I'd better be getting home. I don't want to end up in some ditch. I might be frozen to death before the gritting lorry finds me.'

She laughed, probably as much from relief that he wasn't coming inside as anything else, realising that she hadn't wanted the embarrassment of him and Andrew meeting under these circumstances. 'Thank you, Simon,' she said, 'for a nice evening. It really did me good to get out.' Leaning across, she lightly kissed his cheek, the soft down of his beard strange against her lips.

He sighed, and as she went to get out of the car he said softly, 'Think about trust, Georgina. Keep it at bay for too long and life becomes very empty.'

Moments later she stood on the doorstep, watching as his car ground away up the lane in a swirl of snow. It was all very well for him to talk of trust, almost to imply she should give Andrew another chance and take him back, she thought, but how could she even contemplate that when the question quite simply didn't arise—when it obviously wasn't what Andrew wanted, when he was involved again in yet another relationship?

But what if he wasn't involved? a little voice asked at the back of her mind. What if he wanted to come back to her, wanted her to give their marriage another chance? What then?

But that situation was purely hypothetical so not only did the question not arise it wasn't even worth considering.

As the sound of Simon's car faded into the distance she put her key in the lock, turned it, and as the front door swung open she stepped inside the cottage.

CHAPTER NINE

THE house was quiet and the landing light was burning, which indicated that the girls were in bed. Andrew was sitting on the sofa. He looked up as Georgina came into the room, then switched off the television with the remote control.

'Where's your friend?' he said, glancing beyond her towards the open door.

Georgina, recognising the wary look in his eyes, realised he had expected Simon to come in with her.

'He wouldn't come in,' she said. 'It's snowing—he thought he should get home.' Suddenly she felt weary, deflated almost.

'You didn't enjoy yourself, did you?' said Andrew, staring at her.

'Of course I did,' she replied defensively. 'Whatever makes you think that?'

'Probably years of observing your reactions.' He gave a low chuckle and she looked away. 'I know when you've enjoyed something or not.

'I'll make you some Ovaltine,' he said a moment later, getting to his feet. 'Ovaltine always put things right, didn't it?'

'There's no need,' she said almost sharply. 'I'm perfectly capable of making my own.' But he was gone, out of the room and into the kitchen. With a sigh she followed him and leaned against the doorframe, watching as he put milk into a saucepan and lit the gas.

'I did enjoy it, actually,' she said after a moment. 'The programme was good and the music wonderful. . .'

'But?' He had been about to spoon the Ovaltine

into a mug but he paused and looked at her.

'What do you mean, but?' She frowned.

'I don't know, you tell me. I simply detected a but coming at the end of all that enthusing.'

'Oh, I don't know.' With a helpless little gesture she turned away. 'I guess I've just got out of the habit of going out, socialising. . .I don't know!' she said again, impatiently this time.

'Maybe it's dating you're out of the habit of,' he said, rescuing the saucepan as the milk began to rise then pouring its contents into the mug—stirring as he did so.

'Yes, I dare say it is. . . Perhaps I should have come to you for a few tips.'

His gaze met hers as he passed her the mug. 'Come and sit down,' he said, apparently choosing to ignore the remark and its implications.

They went back into the sitting-room and as Georgina sank down into one of the armchairs, kicking off her shoes as she did so, Andrew sat down on the sofa again but this time he only perched on the edge with his hands linked between his knees.

Georgina sipped the Ovaltine. It tasted wonderful, rich, frothy and very comforting. 'Shouldn't you be going?' she asked after a moment. 'It was snowing quite hard when I came in.'

'Five minutes won't make much difference,' he said in an off-hand sort of way.

'Were the girls all right?' she asked after a little while.

'Yes, fine,' he said, adding, 'At least, to a point they were. They went up all right. . .a bit later than you said, I admit. Then somewhere around ten Natasha started crying out. It sounded as if she was having some sort of a nightmare.'

Georgina sighed. 'She does that sometimes. . .not quite so often now, but still at times. . .'

'I didn't know that—you never told me.' He stared at her.

'What would you have done about it if I had?'

'Well, I don't know,' he admitted. 'But maybe I could have talked to her, helped in some way... When did they start...these nightmares?'

'Soon after you went.'

'Oh. Oh, I see.' He paused as if he didn't know quite what to say next. Georgina suddenly felt a bit sorry for him. After all, it had been she who had insisted he went.

'What did you do? Did you go up to her?' she asked after a moment.

'Yes.' He had been looking at the floor, but he glanced up as he spoke. 'Yes I went up, but by the time I got there Lauren had woken up and she was out of bed and sitting beside Natasha with her arms round her. She put her finger to her lips when she saw me so I waited. Within a few minutes it was all over. Natasha was sleeping again and Lauren got back into her own bed.' He stopped and for a long moment they were both silent. He said, 'You say this happens often?'

'It did,' Georgina said and set her mug down. She added, 'But it's getting less frequent now.'

'Oh, God!' he said, and put his head in his hands.

Georgina watched him for a moment then, getting to her feet, she went and sat beside him and put her hand on his arm. 'Don't, Andrew,' she said softly. 'Don't, please.'

Without looking at her, he covered her hand with his and for a long time they sat there together in the firelight unmoving, both preoccupied with their own thoughts and memories.

When at last they stirred and Andrew opened the front door it was to find that the snow had reached blizzard proportions and the mound of his car resembled an igloo in the icy wastes of the North Pole.

'You can't go home in this,' said Georgina, looking over his shoulder. 'Close the door. I'll get you some blankets and you can sleep on the sofa.' He didn't protest or argue and minutes later she came down with the bedding and helped him to make up his bed.

'I've put a new toothbrush in the bathroom for you,' she said, 'and there's an old bathrobe of mine on the hook behind the door. You can use that if you're cold.'

'Right.' He nodded and stood for a moment, staring down at the sofa.

'I'll go up now and use the bathroom first. Goodnight, Andrew.' Briefly she allowed her eyes to meet his, then immediately looked away again when she saw the expression in his own eyes.

'Goodnight,' he said. As she turned to the door he added, 'Georgina.'

She stopped and answered, without turning. 'Yes?'

'Thank you,' he said, 'for letting me stay.'

She did turn then. 'That's OK,' she said deliberately keeping her voice light. 'It's the least I can do.'

She left, hurrying out of the room and up the stairs. Ten minutes later she lay in bed, listening, as Andrew came up the stairs, just as he had done so many times in the past. Only this time when he'd finished in the bathroom he didn't come into the bedroom, take off his bathrobe and slip naked into bed beside her as he had done so many times before. This time, it was true, he waited for a moment outside her door—a moment when she held her breath, wondering what she would do if he did come in—then he went quietly downstairs and a second later she heard the click of the sitting-room door.

Georgina lay awake for a long time, staring wide-eyed at the ceiling and trying to convince herself that the ache she felt deep inside—an ache that begged for release— had nothing to do with Andrew's presence in the house. How easy it would have been to sleep with him. To allow him to share her bed again, to have him make love to her.

How easy, but how disastrous.

She had spent two long years, nearly three if you counted the time before the divorce, trying to get over Andrew and put her life into some sort of order. She had started to think she was beginning to get somewhere until this last few weeks when seeing him so often again and working alongside him had seemed to reopen all the old wounds. Deep in her heart Georgina had come to the conclusion that she would always love him, and that the feeling she had for him would never really die. Simon had asked her if she'd take Andrew back and had even implied she should trust him again. But could she do that and risk being hurt all over again?

Desperately, as sleep eluded her, all the old questions began to teem in her brain. Andrew had wanted her back once before the divorce, but she had been unable to forgive him for the hurt he had caused her.

Could she forgive him now? And what of Andrew himself? Did he even want her forgiveness now when he had Denise in his life, Denise who quite clearly wanted to settle down, marry and have a family?

Round and round the thoughts went in her head as she grew more and more restless, tossing and turning in the big double bed.

She must have slept at last for the next thing she knew was a light touch on her arm. She opened her eyes and found it was daylight, a strange white daylight, and Andrew was beside the bed, his dark hair tousled from sleep, with a tray of tea in his hands.

She smiled and he smiled back at her, his tender, sexy smile—the one she loved so much.

Then she remembered, and as the mists cleared she struggled to sit up while Andrew set the tray down on the bedside table and sat on the edge of the bed. 'Good morning,' he said softly. 'It's like the Arctic outside.

I thought you might like some tea.'

'Thanks.' She took the mug he handed her and curled her hands around it, too tired to argue with him or remonstrate that he shouldn't really be there, sitting on her bed, at that hour of the morning.

They sipped their tea in companionable silence but before either of them had the chance to say anything more they heard a sound outside on the landing, and the next moment the door was pushed open and Natasha hurtled into the room.

'It snowed! It snowed!' she chanted. 'We'll be able to. . .' She trailed off, her eyes widening as she caught sight of Andrew. 'Daddy!' she shrieked. 'I didn't know you were still here!'

'Hello, poppet.' Andrew set his mug down as Natasha flung herself at him. 'I stayed because it was snowing so hard,' he explained. 'I think Mummy thought it might be too dangerous for me to drive so she said I could sleep here. . .'

'You've got Mummy's dressing-gown on,' spluttered Natasha.

'Well, I didn't have any nightclothes of my own with me so Mummy lent me something of hers,' Andrew replied solemnly.

'So where exactly did you sleep?' a voice from the doorway broke in.

They all looked round and saw Lauren, standing there in her white nightshirt, her hair around her shoulders.

'He slept in the bed with Mummy, of course,' said Natasha, 'just like he used to do, didn't you, Daddy?'

'Actually, poppet, I didn't,' said Andrew, his amused gaze meeting Georgina's. 'I slept downstairs on the sofa.'

'Whatever for?' cried Natasha, bouncing onto the bed. 'I bet it wasn't very nice, was it?'

'It wasn't too bad,' said Andrew, 'although I have to admit I've had a better night's sleep.'

'I know,' said Natasha excitedly. 'Let's all get into the bed now, just like we used to on Sunday mornings— d'you 'member, Daddy?'

'How could I forget?' murmured Andrew.

'Well, come on, then,' ordered Natasha, who by that time had crawled in beside Georgina and had turned back the duvet for Andrew. 'And you, Lauren, come on—all of us together again.'

Georgina, looking at her elder daughter, caught the wary expression in her eyes, but as Andrew climbed into bed beside a giggling Natasha she held out her hand to Lauren. 'Come on, darling,' she said.

Lauren needed no further bidding and she, too, scrambled in between Georgina and Natasha.

After a while Andrew got out again to get a book from the girls' room, and for the next half-hour he read aloud from one of their favourite adventure stories about a white horse with wings.

Eventually when he had finished the story the girls got out of bed—first Natasha, who scrambled to the window to make sure that the snow was still outside and that she hadn't dreamt it and then Lauren, more slowly but nevertheless intrigued at the prospect of all the activities that inevitably followed a fall of snow. The girls went to their room, dressed quickly in jeans and thick jumpers then clattered downstairs.

'Put your Wellingtons on if you go outside,' called Georgina, 'and your coats.'

'Yes, all right,' they yelled back.

She and Andrew lay side by side, listening as Natasha announced she wasn't going to wear gloves as they would get all soggy and Lauren telling her that her hands would turn blue and probably drop off, then came the slamming of the back door, followed by silence.

Neither of them moved or spoke, the situation so unlikely as to beggar belief. At last Andrew broke the silence with a sound that to Georgina, lying rigidly beside him, sounded suspiciously like a chuckle.

Turning her head very carefully, she saw that he was indeed laughing and that the bed itself was beginning to shake beneath them.

'I'm glad you find this funny,' she said weakly at last, but by this time even she was having difficulty keeping a straight face.

'I was just wondering. . .just wondering,' Andrew gasped, 'what your. . .your mother would say if she could see us now. . .'

'I know what she'd say,' said Georgina dryly.

'You do?' Andrew's eyes widened.

'Yes, she'd be shocked.'

'You really think so? Your mum always struck me as being a pretty broadminded sort of person.'

'Oh, she is,' said Georgina, 'but it isn't the circumstances that would shock her—it would be finding you lying there in that fluffy pink dressing-gown that would do it.'

By the time Andrew had finished howling with laughter Georgina had grown serious again. 'No,' she said, 'I doubt Mum would say too much else.'

'I wasn't exactly her favourite person at one time, was I?' said Andrew ruefully.

'No, you weren't,' admitted Georgina. 'But before that she thought the sun shone out of you. . .I guess old habits die hard for some people. . .'

He was silent for a moment then slowly he moved so that he was lying closer to her, so close that she could feel his thigh against hers.

'Do you think,' he said thoughtfully, 'that could be true for most people?'

'What?' She stiffened as a tingle travelled the length of her spine.

'That old habits die hard?'

'I don't know.' She tried to sound casual. 'I wouldn't care to generalise.'

'Maybe we should put the theory to the test.' He turned to her as he spoke and just for one moment Georgina forgot the ludicrousness of the situation—the fact that they were divorced, that he had betrayed and hurt her beyond measure. She even forgot that he was wearing her pink bathrobe.

For that one moment all that mattered was that the man she had once loved with all her heart was lying here beside her in the bed they had once shared, the bed in which they had made love countless times.

'Georgina,' he whispered and, lifting one hand, took a strand of her hair and began to twist it round his finger just like he always used to, at the same time drawing her towards him as he, in turn, moved even closer so that in the end his body was almost covering hers while her face was cupped between his hands with her long hair a wild tangle in his fingers.

'Andrew. . .' She attempted to protest. 'We can't, we mustn't let this happen.' But it sounded feeble even to herself, and at last, completely overwhelmed by his nearness—the hardness of his body signifying his own arousal—and her own ache deep inside, that same ache that had never quite gone away, she was silenced as his mouth covered her own, his tongue questing and seeking, as with a shuddering sigh she gave herself up to him.

Sex between them had always been good right back from the raw, inexperienced passion of their early days through to the finely tuned delight of the years before it had all gone wrong when they had been aware of each other's every need and known how to satisfy it.

Their love-making now, the first after so long, had a kind of desperation about it, as if the pent-up desires and frustrations of the past three years were all released in that one act. As wave after wave of pleasure swept over her Georgina clung to Andrew, but as the frenzy subsided and she lay still and at peace in his arms, the tears still wet on her cheeks, it felt as if she had returned home after some long and very arduous journey.

She lived only for the moment, forgetting the pain of the past and refusing to contemplate what anguish the future might bring, content for this short space of time to have had her immediate needs and desires fulfilled.

They were jolted from their reverie, from the safe, secret world of their dreams, by a shout from the garden.

'Da-ddy! Da-dd-y. Come and see!'

With a sigh, a groan, a final hug and one last kiss, Andrew got up, drawing the pink robe around his body. While Georgina watched him from the bed he crossed to the window and, lifting back the curtain, waved to Natasha.

In the end he stayed to lunch, first shovelling snow from the front path then helping the girls to build a snowman in the back garden of the cottage. To Georgina, as she watched Andrew with the girls from the kitchen window as she cooked the roast—somehow stretching the leg of lamb by adding masses of vegetables—it was as if someone had turned back the clock. And once again she was content for the moment to let it be, knowing it couldn't last but not letting that prospect perturb her in any way.

'That used to be your favourite, Dad, didn't it?' asked Lauren later as they ate the last of the bread-and-butter pudding which, on a sudden impulse, Georgina had made.

'It still is.' Andrew gave a deep sigh of contentment and leaned back in his chair, his eyes meeting Georgina's across the table.

By early afternoon a thaw had set in.

'Oh,' cried Natasha, 'it's melting already. I wanted to go sledging. I wanted Daddy to take us.'

'I have to be getting home,' said Andrew ruefully. 'I have things to do.'

'You could stay again,' said Natasha, but even she didn't sound too hopeful about this, as if it would be stretching luck to impossible lengths.

'No,' said Andrew, 'I have to go, otherwise I won't have a clean shirt for work tomorrow.'

'Thanks for babysitting,' said Georgina when he had managed at last to start his car and was ready to go. She paused, hardly able to meet his gaze, and added, 'And for everything. . .'

'Thank you,' he said looking up at her through the open window of the car, 'for letting me stay. . .and. . . for lunch.'

'That's all right.' Suddenly she felt embarrassed, unable to think what to say next.

'It was great.' His gaze softened. 'Just like it used to be.'

'Yes.' She nodded. 'Yes, it was. I'll. . .I'll see you tomorrow, Andrew.'

He smiled and put the car in gear. 'Bye,' he called. 'See you, girls.' As the car moved a shower of snow sprayed up from the back wheels, and as it ground cautiously up the lane it dislodged great masses of snow from the overhanging branches of the tall conifers.

'That was really nice,' sighed Natasha as they turned to go back into the cottage, 'wasn't it, Mummy?'

'Yes, darling, it was,' agreed Georgina, hoping desperately that she wasn't about to get another third degree from Natasha as to why Andrew couldn't be with them all the time. Then she decided that, on the other hand, maybe that would be preferable to Lauren's silence.

She shouldn't have let it happen, she knew that, because now she was right back at square one and all the careful work she had done in attempting to get over Andrew had been for nothing.

Because now, because of that one moment of weakness in allowing him to make love to her again, it had brought it all back to her. About how wonderful it had always been, how wonderful it still was, how much she still loved him, loved everything about him—his smile, the look of amusement in his dark eyes, the way he kissed her, holding her face, tangling her hair, his lean, hard body, the rhythm of his love-making, the peace when it was over. . .everything. . .everything, damn him! Everything.

But he had hurt her. Could hurt her again. Probably would. Could she stand that again? No! her senses screamed back at her. No, never again. It would kill her a second time.

So, what, then? Where did she go from here? What if Andrew wanted to see her again? What should she say? What should she do? On the other hand, and somehow this seemed even more disturbing, what if he didn't? What if, as far as Andrew was concerned, it had just been a one-off for old times' sake—how would she feel about that?

But wasn't that precisely what it had been for her— a one-off for old times' sake?

Round and round in her mind the questions relentlessly revolved and by the time she got to work the following day she found she was dreading facing him, and when she did there was tension, a tension that almost amounted to coolness between them, leaving Georgina even more confused than before.

'That should be feeling better very soon.' Gently Helen swabbed the boy's head as Andrew inserted the last of eight sutures.

'Will I have a scar?' the boy asked, his lip quivering tremulously again.

'You shouldn't,' said Helen. 'Dr Merrick is very good at needlework, aren't you, Doctor?'

'I do my best,' Andrew replied, 'but I can't promise there won't be any scar at all. That was a nasty argument you had with your dad's garage door, young man.'

'If it does scar,' said Helen, 'you'll just have to grow your hair a little longer in the front to cover it up.' She glanced up as Denny came into the cubicle. 'Ah,' she said, 'here comes Nurse with your anti-tetanus booster.'

She watched as Denny chatted to the boy, before administering the injection. As Andrew straightened up he glanced at his watch and said, 'I must go. Elliot wants me in the treatment room.' He disappeared out of the cubicle without so much as exchanging a glance with Denny.

Helen frowned and a moment later she followed Denny from the cubicle into the nurses' station. The hospital was beginning to show the first effects of a flu epidemic. Several members of staff had already succumbed to the virus, leaving the remainder to cope with full waiting rooms.

Helen had been so busy juggling staff rotas and trying to arrange cover for every shift that she had almost missed the increased tension between Andrew and Georgina. But that morning Georgina's uptight air suggested that something had changed yet again.

Helen called the next patient, a middle-aged woman who had cut her hand on the lid of an empty tin, and escorted her to a vacant cubicle. After taking the woman's particulars, she examined the cut. 'That will require stitching,' she said. 'If you wait a few minutes I will send a doctor in to you.'

Stepping outside the cubicle, she found Denny alone at the desk. 'This is all a bit hectic, isn't it?' she said.

When Denny nodded wearily in reply she went on, 'Never mind, your shift will soon be over.'

Denny nodded again. 'We're supposed to be going to a party tonight,' she said, 'but at this rate I shall be on my knees. I'll have to make the effort, though, because it's Ian's firm's do.'

'Really?' Helen paused, and on a sudden impulse she said, 'All going well between you and Ian?'

'Oh, yes.' Denny smiled happily, her fatigue temporarily forgotten. 'We think we've just found a house.'

'So, does that mean wedding bells soon?'

'Something like that, yes.'

As Denny called yet another patient Helen thoughtfully took herself off to the treatment room to find Andrew.

She bided her time, waiting until he'd sutured the woman's hand and the waiting room was clearer, then, as they took a well-earned, coffee-break in the staff room, she seized the opportunity.

'Andrew,' she said, watching him as he poured his coffee, 'is everything all right?'

'How do you mean, all right?' He glanced up. 'That rather depends to what you are referring. If you mean work then I guess I'm muddling through the same as everyone else—if you mean personally then, well, that's another matter entirely.'

'Does this have anything to do with Georgina?' she said.

'You could say that,' he replied abruptly.

'I thought it might,' she said. 'In a way I feel rather responsible.'

'What do you mean?' Andrew frowned and, perching on the edge of the table, began to sip his coffee.

'It was me who told Georgina about the job here in the first place,' said Helen slowly. 'She was wary, but I persuaded her it wouldn't matter having you two working together again. Maybe I was wrong.'

'I'm not sure it has anything to do with us working together,' said Andrew. 'Although I dare say that may have brought things to a head. But, no, I guess there are things that still need resolving. . .' He trailed off and Helen watched him in silence, not knowing for the moment quite what else to say.

In the end it was Andrew who spoke again, volunteering more information. 'I made a mistake, Helen,' he said tightly, 'a terrible mistake, and I guess I'm paying for it.'

'Maybe some marriages are a mistake,' Helen began uneasily.

Andrew threw her a sharp glance. 'I wasn't referring to my marriage,' he said shortly. 'I meant the divorce, and what led up to it.'

'Oh, oh, I see.' Helen's brain was beginning to teem. Quietly she said, 'What are you saying, Andrew?'

'That I still love her,' he replied simply.

She stared at him. 'And have you told her that?'

'No,' he said, 'because I'm afraid of what her reaction will be.'

'You hurt her badly.'

'You think I don't know that?' He pushed himself away from the table, set down his mug and strode to the window, where he stood staring out at the fields beyond the hospital and the downs in the distance, their tops still covered with snow.

'Like I said,' he went on after a moment, without turning round, 'I made a mistake. I had an affair. . .no, I can't even call it that. It was a fling. An infatuation, no more than that. I don't even know why I did it. I've agonised over that, and I can only come up with the fact that it was at a time when Georgina was so desperate to get back to work. . .'

'And you were against that?'

'At the time I was. Yes,' Andrew admitted honestly. 'I couldn't see it was necessary. She'd been forced to

work after Lauren was born because we were desperate
for the money, but by the time Natasha came along I felt
I wanted to provide for my family.'

'You didn't consider Georgina's need to resume her
career?'

'No, I don't suppose I did. I can see now that was
wrong. Anyway, we drifted apart a bit and I guess I
was feeling hard-done-by. She was so involved with the
girls. . .

'That's not an excuse.' He turned sharply as Helen
would have intervened, 'but it's an explanation, brutal
and inadequate as it is. . .and it's the only one, as far as
I can see. I'm not proud of what I did, Helen. I gave in
to flattery. I betrayed Georgina and everything we had
built up. And I used Rachel, even though she was more
than willing. . .' He trailed off again and moodily
returned to the view beyond the window.

'Andrew.' Helen hesitated, choosing her words with
care. 'Have you told Georgina any of this?'

'Yes, of course. . . At least, I tried to. . .'

'When?'

'What do you mean, when?'

'When exactly did you try to tell her all this?'

'Well, at the time, I suppose. . . After she found out
about Rachel. . . When she said she wanted a divorce. . .'

'When she was still feeling raw? When she probably
felt she hated you for what you had done to her and to
the girls?'

'Yes, I guess so.'

'Have you tried again since?'

'Not really.' He paused. 'I suppose there has been the
odd occasion when I could have done, especially since
she's come here to work. But, it's like I said, I'm not
sure what her reaction would be. I have an awful feeling
she wouldn't want to know.'

'You won't know, Andrew, unless you try. And,

who knows, you may just be surprised?'

He turned sharply from the window and stared at her, and Helen could not help but see the hope that leapt in his dark eyes. 'You think——?'

'I don't know, Andrew. I really don't,' she interrupted him. 'But Georgina has had time to cool down now. She has had a period of time apart from you, alone with the girls, a time for reflection. Where forgiveness might once have been impossible maybe now. . . Who knows?'

She stood up, draining her own mug as she did so. 'There are, however,' she went on briskly, 'a couple of things that you really will have to do if you are cherishing any hopes at all of getting Georgina back.'

'Yes?' he said, his eagerness almost boyish. 'And what are they?'

'Well,' Helen replied carefully, 'the first is that you will have to take things very slowly and woo her all over again.'

'That shouldn't be too difficult.' Andrew forced a smile. 'And the second?'

'You will have to tell Georgina you aren't in a relationship with Denise White,' said Helen crisply.

'Denise White?' He frowned blankly. 'I don't understand. I never have been in a relationship with her.'

Helen smiled. 'I know that and so do you. But, unfortunately, Georgina thinks otherwise so before you do anything else, Andrew, you really do need to put the record straight.'

CHAPTER TEN

'How are you feeling, Emily?' It was two days later. Georgina had just attended a lecture on the third floor of the hospital which was close to the orthopeadic unit, and on a sudden impulse she had called in to see Emily Sanderson. Propped up by pillows and a back-rest, Emily was reading a rather elderly copy of *National Geographic*, but as Georgina spoke she peered up at her over the top of her glasses.

'Now where do I know you from?' she asked with a frown. 'I know your face but I can't quite place you... there are so many of you in here...'

'I'm Georgina Merrick,' said Georgina with a smile. 'I was on duty in Casualty when you were brought in.'

'That's right,' said Emily crisply. 'I thought I knew your face. And weren't you the one who came in to see me later with...with my son?'

Georgina nodded. 'Yes.' She paused, then said, 'And how is Tommy?'

'Having a whale of a time, from what I can make out,' Emily sniffed. 'I don't know, you worry yourself sick over them and all the time...' Leaving the sentence unfinished, she peered closely at Georgina again. 'Do you have children?' she asked.

'Yes,' Georgina replied, 'I have two girls.'

'And how old are they?'

'Seven and ten.'

Emily sighed. 'About the same as Tommy.' She paused and added, 'The difference being that yours, presumably, will grow up.' Briefly her gaze met Georgina's then she looked away.

'You say Tommy is happy where he is?' Georgina asked after a moment.

'He appears to be,' Emily replied rather stiffly.

'Maybe,' said Georgina carefully, knowing she was treading on thin ice, 'you will find he will be happy to mix a little more in the future.' Emily remained silent, her mouth drawn into a thin line. 'And you'll be glad of some help until your hip is completely strong again,' Georgina added.

'Why don't you come right out with it, young woman, and say what you mean?' Suddenly Emily's eyes were glittering behind her glasses.

'I'm sorry.' Georgina was taken aback. 'I don't know what you. . .'

'Yes, you do,' snapped Emily. 'You're like all the rest—you think Tommy should be in care. And you're wondering what will happen to him when I die.'

'I can assure you—' Georgina began, but Emily cut her short again.

'I've always managed Tommy. He's my son, and I promised my husband before he died that I wouldn't let anyone take Tommy away. He's perfectly happy with me but the do-gooders wouldn't see that, interfering, meddling lot.'

'Is that why you've kept Tommy indoors since you came here to live?' asked Georgina curiously.

Emily's face took on an even more stubborn expression. 'What they didn't see they wouldn't know about,' she snapped. 'We managed and we were quite happy, just the two of us.'

'I'm sure you were, Emily,' said Georgina gently. 'And probably that was fine. . .until you needed help. . . until the unforseen happened.' She glanced down as she spoke at the blanket that covered Emily's legs and when Emily maintained her stubborn silence she said, 'So where exactly is Tommy at the moment?'

'In some residential home for the mentally handicapped, but he's coming back just as soon as I get home.'

'Yes, Emily, of course he is. . .but. . .' Georgina
hesitated.

'But what? What are you suggesting?' Emily looked
up sharply at Georgina.

'Nothing, really. I was simply wondering if it might
not be a good idea for Tommy to attend a day centre
sometimes.'

'Why?' demanded Emily suspiciously.

'Only so that if the unforeseen did happen again, and
you were unable to care for him, he would be familiar
with another place, with other people and a different
routine and it wouldn't come as such a shock to him.'

Emily took off her glasses and frowned but Georgina
could see that she was interested and not about to dismiss
the idea out of hand. 'Would they do that—just let him
go on a daily basis?' she asked at last.

Georgina nodded. 'I understand that is what happens.'

Emily gave a deep sigh. 'I always imagined that if he
got involved with something like that they would take
over and I'd lose him completely.'

'I'm sure that wouldn't be the case, Emily,' Georgina
said gently. 'And if you agreed to it I think you would
find that both you and Tommy would benefit enormously.
Tommy because the activities would occupy and stimu-
late him, and you because. . .well, because it would give
you a break, and you can't tell me that sometimes you
wouldn't be glad of a break. I know I am. . .the girls can
be hard work at times and very demanding. . .' Her gaze
met Emily's again and what she saw there this time was
understanding and agreement.

'Will you give it a try?' she asked after a moment.

Emily pursed her lips. 'I'll think about it,' she said.

That had to suffice for the time being but as Georgina
took her leave of Emily she felt she had made at least

some headway in this rather unusual domestic situation.

Talking to Emily had made her late for her next shift but as she hurried through the nurses' station of the orthopaedic ward she was hailed by a shout from one of the smaller, four-bedded wards. Whoever it was had called her by name, not simply a summons to any passing nurse, and as Georgina stopped in her tracks and moved back to the ward she saw Jack Oakley in the corner bed, waving cheerily to her.

'Hello, Jack!' Delighted to see him looking so much better in spite of the plaster casts on both legs, Georgina, her haste forgotten, came right into the ward.

'I thought it was you just now when you first came in,' said Jack. 'They've moved you up here now, have they?' He looked hopeful and Georgina laughed.

'No, Jack, no such luck. I've been attending a lecture and I called in here to see someone. And now I'm glad that I did because I've seen you as well, and I'll be able to report back to the rest of the Casualty team about how much better you are looking.'

'Well, I'm a mass of pins and tubes but I'm getting there,' said Jack with a grin, 'and the important thing is they saved me legs. . .quite a man, that Mr Baltimore.'

'Yes, Jack, he is,' agreed Georgina. 'You'll be driving that tractor again before you know it.'

'Maybe. . .but not right away.' He gave a sheepish grin. 'The wife's put her foot down. Some sort of holiday first, or so she says. . .'

'I agree entirely,' said Georgina firmly.

'You women always stick together,' said Jack.

'It's what you need, Jack, both of you.'

'That may well be.' Jack pulled a face. 'But can you see it? Me on a cruise! Foreign ports, foreign food. Fancy clothes and not a tractor or a milking machine in sight. Honestly, Nurse, I ask you. Can you see it?'

Georgina was still chuckling when she got back to A and E.

'What's tickled you?' asked Dot curiously when Georgina joined her in the nurses' station.

'I've been to see Jack Oakley,' Georgina explained. 'He's such a character.'

'Well, I wish I had time to go visiting,' sighed Dot, rolling her eyes, 'but some of us have to work.'

'OK, OK,' Georgina laughed, 'I know I'm late. I'm sorry, but I'm here now.'

'That dishy blond guy was in here earlier,' said Dot, eyeing her up and down.

'Blond guy?' asked Georgina faintly, knowing full well to whom Dot was referring.

'Yes, that locum from the centre. . .asking for you, he was. Elliot told him you were at a lecture and he said he'd catch you later.'

'Oh,' said Georgina. 'Oh, I see.' She'd been feeling a bit guilty about Simon, knowing she should really have contacted him to thank him for the evening at the theatre but at the same time vaguely concerned that if she did so he might misconstrue the gesture into thinking that she wanted a follow-up date. Even as she wondered what she would say to him Helen looked out of her office.

'Oh, there you are, Georgina,' she said. 'Andrew was looking for you earlier.'

'I'm getting really sick of this,' said Dot. 'What's she got that the rest of us haven't, for goodness' sake? She's hardly been in the place five minutes and she's got every male in sight lusting after her.'

'Not quite,' said Helen drily. 'Norman Westwood was looking for you just now, Dot.'

'And that wasn't because he's lusting after my body— it's because he wants me to take part in some sponsored swim,' said Dot in disgust. 'I've been avoiding him all day.'

'Ah, well, you can't have it all ways,' said Helen. 'You have to take the rough with the smooth where these men are concerned.'

'Did Andrew say what he wanted?' asked Georgina. Helen shook her head and went back into her office.

'You two getting it together again?' asked Dot curiously as they made their way to the treatment rooms.

'Oh, no,' said Georgina quickly, so quickly that Dot raised her eyebrows in surprise.

'I only wondered, that's all.' she said defensively.

'I expect he wanted to ask something about the girls,' said Georgina weakly. She'd hardly seen Andrew since the night he had spent at the cottage, but she doubted whether he'd been out of her thoughts for more than a second or two the entire time. It wasn't deliberate, her thinking about him, it just happened. Somehow he was just there with every breath she took, with every thought that entered her head.

'So, what did the other one want?' asked Dot, pushing open the treatment room door.

'Other one?' asked Georgina vaguely, her pulse suddenly quickening as she realised that Andrew was in the room attending to a patient on one of the beds.

'Yes,' said Dot, lowering her voice, 'the blond one. That could hardly have been about the girls, could it?'

'No.' Georgina paused. 'Maybe it was something to do with the concert. . .'

'What concert?' Dot had started to strip the second of the treatment room beds, which had just been vacated, but she stopped and stared at Georgina.

'The one he took me to on Saturday evening,' said Georgina, wishing that Dot would shut up because Andrew was quite obviously listening to every word they said.

'Let's get this straight,' said Dot. 'Are you saying that blond gladiator actually took you out?'

Georgina nodded, her gaze flickering to Andrew who still had his back to them.

'Well,' Dot almost exploded. 'All I can say is that not only do you get all the luck but you are a dark horse into the bargain. Why didn't you tell us?'

'There wasn't really anything to tell. . .'

'Oh, come on,' said Dot, her voice taking on a scornful note. 'I wasn't born yesterday, you know. He's absolutely gorgeous. What was he like—?'

Georgina was saved from answering and from any further interrogation from Dot by Elliot, who suddenly appeared in the treatment room doorway.

'Road traffic accident arriving in five minutes,' he said abruptly. 'Car and a lorry in a collision at Coppins Bridge. One fatality, two seriously injured. Are you ready in here?'

'Yes, Elliot,' said Georgina, her gaze, as he straightened up and turned from the bed, meeting Andrew's for the first time since she had come into the room.

The injuries from the road traffic accident kept the staff in the treatment room fully occupied for the remainder of that particular shift. The lorry driver had escaped serious injury and was cared for in one of the cubicles, but the occupants of the car involved in the same accident did not fare so lightly. The young driver had died at the scene in Dave Morey's arms as the paramedic had fought desperately to save him, and now it was the turn of the A and E staff to try to save the lives of two of his passengers.

'He was only a kid,' said Dave to Georgina and Dot as they set up saline drips and applied oxygen masks. 'They're all just kids. On a lunchtime jaunt from school, by the looks of it, in the lad's Mini.'

The girls, indeed, were still wearing school uniforms, the white blouses grimy now and spattered with blood and the short skirts revealing hopelessly laddered tights. One girl was sobbing and crying noisily while the other, her long blonde hair damp with blood, was strangely silent.

Swiftly but carefully clothing was cut away and injuries assessed. In both cases these was loss of blood from open wounds inflicted by jagged metal, limbs fractured from the impact, breathing difficulties from the more silent of the two girls and mounting hysteria from the other.

Andrew was joined by Susan Jollife and assisted by Elliot, Helen, Georgina and Dot the two doctors worked over the young victims.

Gradually Susan and Dot calmed the more distraught of the two girls. Then, as Georgina had just finished phoning X-Ray, there came a shout from Andrew who was working on the other girl.

'She's arrested! Get her into Resusc.'

By the time Georgina had slammed the phone down the girl's bed had been wheeled into the resuscitation room, and when she joined them Andrew had already begun cardiac massage and Susan was inserting an airway, while Helen, at Andrew's instruction, began drawing up lignocaine and adrenaline.

Georgina attached monitor pads to the girl's chest and as the cardiac massage continued all eyes turned anxiously to the monitor screen. The line, however, remained ominously straight.

'Defib,' rapped Andrew after several agonising moments.

Georgina had already anticipated this and was standing by with the defibrillator. As the pads were applied to the girl's chest Andrew ordered everyone to stand clear, and a shock was administered in an attempt to start her heart again.

The monitor line, however, stayed stubbornly still

without so much as a flicker to signify that life was present.

'Again,' said Andrew between gritted teeth 'Stand clear!'

Still there was no response, and a subsequent attempt also proved to no avail.

'We've lost her,' said Andrew at last. 'Damn it, we've lost her.' A look of helpless frustration on his face, he checked for the pulse that wasn't there.

'No!' said Georgina, staring in disbelief at the girl who lay before them with her blonde hair spread across the pillow, her lips already blue in a chalk-white face. 'She's too young...can't we try a bit longer?' She had to swallow to disperse the panic-stricken sob that had risen in her throat.

'I'm sorry,' said Andrew quietly, his eyes on Georgina's face. 'She's gone. Thank you all.' He glanced round at the others who mumbled responses, cleared throats or busied themselves with the tasks that had to be done.

Sick at heart, Georgina turned away, her feelings a mixture of frustration that they had lost the girl, anguish that she had died at such an early age and anger that the incident had upset her so much. She really should be used to this sort of thing by now, even if she had been away from nursing for so long.

By the time they trailed disconsolately back into the treatment room it was to find that the other girl had been taken to X-Ray and Dot was clearing up the mess. She looked up as they approached, one glance at their faces enough to tell her what had happened. 'Helen,' she said, glancing tentatively at the sister, 'the parents are here... will you?'

'Yes,' Helen sighed and took a deep breath. 'Yes, of course. God, how I hate this bit.'

'I'll come with you,' said Andrew.

'Thanks.' Helen shot him a grateful look and together they disappeared in the direction of the privacy of her office.

'You all right?' asked Dot as Georgina, her hands shaking, automatically began to help her.

'Yes.' She nodded. 'I think so. . . It's just that she was so young. . .no more than fourteen I should think. . .not much older than Lauren.'

'Look, why don't you go and get yourself a cup of tea?' said Dot briskly. 'I can manage in here.'

'No, really, I'm all right,' said Georgina shakily. She didn't feel all right but she didn't want to appear a wimp in front of Dot.

'For once why don't you just do as you're told?' Dot's gaze met hers.

'All right.' With her head down, Georgina hurried away.

Dave Morey and Pete Steel were in the staff canteen. After Georgina had bought herself a cup of tea and taken it to a table by the window, Dave came across to her.

'Did she make it,' he asked, 'the little blonde one?'

Unable to speak, Georgina shook her head.

Dave stared at her then, in a gesture of utter helplessness, ran his hand over his short dark hair. 'Jeez,' he muttered, half turning away to hide his obvious distress. 'What a waste. . .they were kids. . .that's all, kids. . .the lad was only seventeen. . . Why the hell do these things have to happen. . .?' He trailed off, struggling for control. As Georgina furiously stirred the non-existent sugar in her tea he said, 'What about the other girl?'

'She was OK.' At last Georgina found her voice. 'She's in X-Ray, but there was nothing that won't mend.'

'She was lucky,' said Dave. 'She was sitting behind the passenger—he was all right, too, but the other one was behind the driver. They copped the lot because the whole of that side of the car was ripped off. Anyway. . .'

he paused '. . .thanks for letting me know. I'll go and tell Pete. He's pretty cut up about the whole thing as well.' With a brief nod he made his way back to his table to give the grim news to his colleague.

'I was told I might find you here.' A familiar voice at her elbow made Georgina look up to find Andrew by her side. 'Can I join you?'

She nodded and he sat down opposite her and placed his own cup of tea on the table.

'Are you OK?' he asked after a moment, and when she looked up it was to find his dark eyes full of concern. It was Georgina's undoing and helplessly she felt her own eyes fill with tears.

'No,' she said, 'I'm not. I'm a disgrace to the nursing profession and an utter wimp.'

'No, you're not,' he said softly. 'I would be far more suspicious of a nurse who didn't show compassion than of one who did.'

'Even so. . .' She gave a shrug and blinked rapidly to clear her eyes, hating herself for showing such weakness.

'We couldn't have done any more, you know, back there,' he said after a while. 'We could have gone on for another hour but it wouldn't have made any difference.'

'I know.' She looked up sharply. 'Oh, I know that, Andrew, really I do. It was just that. . .just that she was so young and. . . Oh. . .I don't know really what I mean. . .'

'I do,' said Andrew. 'I know exactly. You were thinking of the girls and how we would feel if that had been one of them. You were thinking that if it had been one of them would I have tried for longer—?'

'Andrew—'

'Yes, you were. I know you were,' he said gently. 'And the answer is no. It would not have done any good.'

'The parents. . .?' Fearfully again her gaze met his.

'Devastated, of course.'

They were silent for a while after that but at last

Georgina spoke. 'I still shouldn't have been so weak,' she said. 'I guess I'm just going to have to toughen up a bit in future.'

'Well, if needing a cup of tea is being weak then I'm guilty of it as well because I certainly was in great need of one.' Draining his cup, Andrew stood up then he looked down at her and said, 'Actually, I was looking for you earlier. Helen said you were in a lecture. I was wondering—I've got some stuff for Lauren for her project. Could I drop it over this evening?'

'Yes, of course.' She heard herself answer without a second thought. This wasn't keeping to the weekend arrangements that they had agreed upon at the time of the divorce, she thought as she watched Andrew walk away, but after the enormity of what had just happened a little thing like that somehow seemed of very little consequence.

The girls, of course, were delighted to see him so unexpectedly. Georgina, quite deliberately, hadn't told them he was coming and his arrival after tea, while they were doing their homework, was heralded by shrieks of surprise.

'Have you eaten?' asked Georgina after he'd given Lauren the material for her project.

Andrew shook his head. 'No, I was going to grab a take-away on the way home.'

'There's some lasagne left,' she said, 'and a bit of salad. You're welcome to that—I made too much.'

Even as he hesitated Natasha said, 'Mummy always makes too much. She says she still cooks for four.'

As she met Andrew's eye Georgina gave an embarrassed little shrug.

'Old habits again?' he said softly.

'Something like that.' She tried to appear casual, offhand, but feared she failed miserably, knowing he was referring to the last time he had been here in the cottage with her while the girls had been playing outside in the snow.

She turned to the fridge and began taking lettuce and tomatoes from the salad box. She mustn't think about that now, she thought desperately, because if she did Andrew would be sure to know and maybe, heaven forbid, would even begin to suspect just how much she had enjoyed it. She couldn't let that happen. If she did she would be right back at square one and all the careful building up of a life without Andrew would have been for nothing.

'Daddy,' she heard Natasha say through the open door of the sitting-room, 'when can we go skating again?'

'When you like,' Andrew replied. 'Next weekend, if that's all right with Mummy. The only thing is, it looks as if we are going to have to manage without Denise in future.'

Georgina had been about to put the portion of lasagne into the microwave but she paused and stiffened at the mention of Denise.

'Why?' Natasha demanded.

'Well, it looks like she's going to be pretty busy on Saturdays from now on and not have time to go ice-skating,' Andrew replied.

'Why will she be busy? What does she have to do?' Natasha quite obviously could not perceive that anything could be more important than ice-skating on a Saturday afternoon.

'She's bought a new house,' said Andrew, 'and she and her fiancé have a lot to do to get it ready to live in.'

Georgina stared at the microwave.

'What's a fiancé?' asked Natasha.

'Don't you know anything?' Lauren's voice was scornful. 'It's the person you're going to marry, isn't it, Dad?'

'Yes, it is,' Andrew agreed.

'So who is Denise going to marry?' Natasha obviously hadn't finished.

'A young man by the name of Ian,' said Andrew.

'Oh, poor Daddy,' said Natasha. 'You must be dreadfuly upset.'

'Why should I be upset, poppet?' There was a definite note of amusement in Andrew's voice now, and Georgina found herself holding her breath.

'Well, I was when Joey Saunders said he didn't want to be my boyfriend any more,' said Natasha solemnly, 'and Denise was your girlfriend, Daddy, wasn't she?'

'I don't know what gave you that idea.' Andrew laughed.

'She was always there.' It was Lauren who answered, and there was a decided note of accusation in her tone.

'Always where?' asked Andrew.

'When we went skating,' Natasha chipped in.

'Exactly,' said Andrew. 'Denise is a very good skater and, in case you hadn't noticed, I'm a not very good skater. . .'

'Pretty bad, really,' said Natasha.

'Not that bad,' Andrew protested.

'You kept falling over.'

'Did I? Yes, well, I suppose I did. Anyway, that's why Denise used to come with us. She knew I couldn't skate, and when I told her that you two were keen to learn she offered to come along and teach you. I think that was very good of her to give up her Saturday afternoons like that, don't you?'

'Yes, it was,' agreed Natasha.

'Did she know you couldn't cook either?' asked Lauren.

'What do you mean?' Andrew sounded indignant.

'Well, she used to come back to the flat afterwards and cook our tea,' replied Lauren crisply.

As Andrew laughed Georgina let go of the breath she had been holding, opened the microwave door and popped the lasagne inside.

CHAPTER ELEVEN

LATER, when Georgina looked back, she realised it was around that time that things began to change. At first the changes were barely perceptible—Andrew's unscheduled visits, which became more and more frequent until in the end his presence at the cottage was almost taken for granted and hardly a cause for comment, or the way he just happened to appear when she needed help, whether it was with the girls and their homework, when her car broke down or when the pipe from the bathroom froze in the icy January weather.

He made no further advances to her of an intimate or sexual nature and where at first she was relieved, not knowing how she would handle it if he did, as time went on it began, very slightly, to disturb her. Was it that he no longer found her attractive—that the one time they had made love had been a mistake—that he had regretted it?

But if that was the case why was he around so much? She wasn't certain how she'd felt about finding out that Denise White was not and never had been his girlfriend. It certainly meant that Andrew was uninvolved romantically but it didn't alter the fact that he had been romantically involved elsewhere while he had been married to her and neither did it alter the circumstances of their divorce.

It was a cold winter, uncharacteristic of the Island with its usually temperate climate, with several icy spells as January at last lurched into a bleak February. Georgina saw little of Simon Phillips during this time but whenever his name was mentioned or she caught a glimpse of the big, blond figure in the nearby Fleetwood Centre she was forced to fight a pang of guilt. She had not contacted him since their evening out, neither had he attempted to see her again, and she could only conclude that he had found her company so boring that he didn't wish to repeat the excercise.

Then late one afternoon as she was coming off her shift she almost bumped into him in the hospital foyer.

'Georgina!' His eyes lit up and he seemed genuinely pleased to see her. 'How are you?'

'I'm well, Simon, thank you. And you?' She scanned his features and found that she, too, was glad to see him again.

'Yes, fine. I've just been up to the wards to see a patient. Are you in a hurry or do you have time for a quick drink?'

'Well. . .' She hesitated. 'I should be getting home, really, but. . .'

'Just a quick one in the social club. I. . . There's something I'd like to tell you. . .'

'You've got me intrigued now.' She laughed at him. 'So how can I refuse?'

The club was almost deserted at that early hour and after Simon had bought a drink for them both they sat at a table to one side of the bar in a little alcove.

'Cheers!' He raised his glass, took a sip of his drink, set his glass down and then smiled at her. 'It really is good to see you again, you know.'

'And you,' she replied, sipping her own drink and realising that she really meant it. 'Actually, Simon, I've been feeling a bit guilty,' she said carefully.

'You have?' He looked mystified.

'Yes, I should have contacted you after the concert. I meant to, but somehow. . .well, the time just slipped by and. . .'

'Don't worry about it. It doesn't matter, really it

doesn't. Besides, I expect you've been busy.'

'That's no excuse.' Georgina shook her head. 'I always impress on my girls that they must say thank you and here I am, breaking my own rule and setting a bad example into the bargain. Anyway, I really did enjoy it so I'll say thank you now, if it isn't too late.'

'Of course it isn't.' He took another sip of his drink and then when he remained silent Georgina looked curiously at him.

'You said you have something to tell me,' she said at last.

'Yes, I do.' He nodded and appeared to be struggling to find the right words. For one moment Georgina thought he was going to ask her out again, and found herself wondering how she could refuse without hurting his feelings. She liked him, but the last thing she wanted was for him to get any ideas. He'd been hurt once and she didn't want to be the one to do it again.

'I went away last weekend,' he said at last.

She stared at him. She wasn't sure what she had been expecting him to say but it wasn't that.

'I went back to Oxford,' he went on, 'where I was living before I came here. I went to see Michelle. . .'

'The girl you were living with?'

'Yes.'

'Ah.'

He remained silent for a long moment, toying with the handle of his pint mug, then he looked up at Georgina and said, 'It was because of you that I went.'

'Me?' She stared at him in astonishment. 'I don't understand. Whatever did I have to do with it?'

'It was something you said,' he replied slowly. 'That night we went out. When I told you about Michelle and how we had lived together for nearly four years, you said it must have been like being married. I couldn't get that out of my head afterwards. I know you'll think I was daft but I even came here to the hospital one day to talk to you again. . .to ask your advice. . .I suppose, to get the woman's point of view. . .' He shrugged, then went on, 'Anyway, you weren't here, but I carried on thinking about it and in the end I came to the conclusion that you were absolutely right and that, yes, it had been exactly like being married, and that I'd been a fool to let all that, and Michelle, go so easily.'

Georgina stared at him, lost for words.

'There was another thing,' he said after a moment. 'I couldn't help but notice how sad you seemed about the break-up of your own marriage and how, deep down, you seemed still to care so much for your ex-husband.' He hesitated, throwing her a tentative glance. 'At least, that was the impression you gave, and it set me thinking about myself and Michelle. So much so that I finally came to the conclusion that I really did still love her, and that I would give anything for things to be back the way they had been between us.'

'So, what happened?' Georgina leaned forward slightly, eager now to learn the outcome.

'As I said,' Simon went on, 'I went back to Oxford to see her. She had been as miserable as me since the break-up. Her other relationship had ended almost as soon as it had begun and she was on her own. To cut a long story short, we are going to give ourselves another chance when I go back to take up my new post in the spring.'

'Oh, Simon, I'm so pleased.' Georgina clasped her hands together in delight. 'I really am. It's so nice these days to hear a story that has a happy ending.'

Leaning back in his chair, he surveyed her through narrowed eyes. 'So, what about your story?' he said.

'What about my story?' She tried to keep her tone light.

'Could that also not have a happy ending?'

'In what way? It's a bit different for me, Simon. Andrew and I are divorced.'

'But surely that doesn't necessarily mean the end of a story.'

'I don't know, Simon,' she said, a frown creasing her forehead. 'I don't think what you are suggesting could be possible.'

He was silent for a moment, as if in deep reflection, then he said, 'When we talked before you implied that trust would be a problem for you.'

'Are you saying it won't be for you?' she asked carefully, her gaze meeting his.

'Not at all,' he replied, his voice soft now and his gaze holding hers. 'I don't doubt it will be a problem, but I'm prepared to give it a chance. Like I told you before, life can be very empty if you don't sometimes take a chance.'

'Maybe what I need is to speak to someone who has taken that chance and proved it can work,' said Georgina.

'Maybe you do,' Simon agreed.

'The problem will be finding someone,' Georgina remarked dryly.

At the end of February Andrew told them that he had to attend a medical conference in London.

'How long will you be away?' wailed Natasha.

'Only a week,' Andrew replied. 'I shall be back next Sunday.'

'Will you drive up?' asked Georgina.

'No.' He shook his head. 'I'll go on the train.'

'We'll take you to the ferry, won't we, Mum?' said Lauren.

'I was hoping you'd say that,' Andrew smiled.

'I don't like Daddy being away,' said Natasha on the following Saturday morning as she and Lauren prepared to go to the stables. 'He comes to see us much more now, doesn't he, Mummy?'

'Yes, he does,' Georgina agreed, and added, 'He'll be home tomorrow night.'

'Will he come to see us then?' asked Lauren hopefully.

'I don't know,' Georgina replied. 'It might be too late.'

'Well, I hope he does,' said Natasha. 'I really miss him. Do you miss him, Mummy?'

'It certainly seems strange with him away,' replied Georgina guardedly. What she didn't say as the girls ran ahead of her and scrambled into the car was that, yes, she, too, had missed Andrew in the short time he had been away. She had missed his presence at work, his voice on the phone—even though he had phoned once 'to speak to the girls'—but even more she had missed his visits to the cottage, the way he would turn up unexpectedly, joining them for a meal or to sit around the fire in the evening. And, yes, she, too, would be glad when he came home.

It had been a grey, damp, miserable week, but that morning had dawned crisp and bright with a breeze that, although chilly, was only light. The girls were excited by the prospect of a day-long hack over the downs and they chattered non-stop on the short drive to the riding stables.

Other children had already arrived when they drove into the yard and several horses were tacked up and ready to go, their hot breath hanging in the cold morning air and their hooves striking the cobbles as they pawed the ground, anxious to be away. Jean Mitchell, the proprietor, in jodhpurs and tweed jacket, greeted Georgina with a shout and a raised riding crop.

'Mrs Merrick! So pleased the girls could make it. Promises to be a good day.' She spoke in short, staccato, sentences, ending with a sharp bark of a laugh.

Georgina waited until the horses the girls were to ride

were tacked up and they were mounted—Lauren on
Dolly, a sleek grey, and Natasha on Conker, the frisky
little chestnut pony she so loved to ride. She watched as
girths were tightened and instructions given, then the line
of horses moved away, some slipping slightly on the
damp cobbles as they filed beneath the stone archway
out of the stable yard and into the lane which led to the
bridle paths and open downland. Lauren, looking elegant
and confident, raised her crop as she passed, while
Natasha's excited little face peeped out at Georgina from
beneath the peak of her pink and mauve helmet.

Then they were gone, the sound of the horses' hooves
soon only an echo in the still February morning.

With a sigh, and quite suddenly feeling more lonely
than ever, Georgina walked back to her car, glad that her
mother had asked her to lunch—that there was at least
one thing to help fill the void of her empty day.

'I hear Andrew visits a lot these days,' her mother said
as she poured a sherry for Georgina.

'You've been gossiping with Natasha,' sniffed
Georgina, leaning back and letting her hand drop to
fondle the velvety head of Saracen, her mother's black
cat, as he rubbed himself around the legs of her chair.

'Natasha doesn't usually let me down.' Lorna Bailey
smiled and sipped her own sherry. They were sitting in
her conservatory enjoying the first of the spring sunshine
while they waited for the lunch to cook. 'She also tells
me,' Lorna went on after a moment, 'that you went to a
concert with a man with a golden beard. Was that,' she
said, throwing her daughter a shrewd glance, 'a one-off
experience or one that is likely to be repeated?'

'Oh, a one-off,' said Georgina firmly. 'Yes, definitely
a one-off.'

'Can I take it that the experience was not an enjoyable
one?' Quizzically Lorna raised one eyebrow.

'Oh, it was enjoyable. . .to a point.'

'But not worth repeating. . .?'

'Let's say, not likely to be repeated.' Georgina paused. 'Don't get me wrong. Simon is a lovely man but he'd been in a long-term relationship which had recently ended. He's since told me they are going to try again. . . that they still love each other. . .'

'Ah, I see,' said Lorna. 'Prepared to give love a second chance, is that it?'

'Something like that, I suppose,' said Georgina. All at once without exactly knowing why she felt more lonely and more miserable than ever. 'I only hope she doesn't hurt him again, that it works out this time,' she added almost fiercely.

'Well, he'll never know if he doesn't give it a chance,' said Lorna.

'It isn't easy trying to trust someone again once that trust has been betrayed,' Georgina said sharply.

'I know,' replied Lorna.

'You don't, Mum,' Georgina retorted, shaking her head. 'No one can know unless they've experienced it. . .'

'Maybe not, and maybe I haven't experienced it in quite the way you think, but—'

'Dad always adored you,' Georgina went on heatedly. 'You can't possibly understand.'

'I know your father adored me. I also know he never stopped loving or trusting me.' Lorna paused. Setting her glass down on the white wrought-iron table, she added, 'Even after I'd betrayed that trust.'

Thinking she must have misheard, Georgina stared at her mother, wondering what on earth she was talking about.

'Oh, yes, I betrayed his trust, you know.' Lorna threw Georgina a rueful glance. When her daughter remained speechless she went on, 'It was many, many years ago when you were still a child, and it happened with a

colleague of your father's. Don't ask me why it happened
because I couldn't tell you—something to do with me
feeling neglected while your father worked long hours,
something to do with flattery and lots of attention, I
presume. . .'

She paused again, for a long moment this time, and
then, without looking at Georgina, she went on, 'I'm not
particularly proud of what happened and. . .I can honestly
say I don't think I ever stopped loving your father. But
that's neither really here nor there. The point I'm making,
Georgina. . .' she glanced up, her gaze briefly meeting
that of her daughter '. . .is that anyone is capable of
making a mistake. I know—I did. But if your father
hadn't found it in his heart to forgive me, to go on loving
me and trusting me, the thirty or so happy years we spent
together afterwards would never have happened. . .'

She trailed off and stood up. 'I must go and see to
the lunch,' she said, and with eyes that were suddenly
suspiciously bright from the effort of what she had
revealed and the memories it had evoked she hurried into
the house, leaving Georgina stunned and alone in the
conservatory.

She could hardly believe what her mother had told
her. She had always lived in the belief that her mother
could have no real understanding of her own situation,
having had no experience of what it was like to have
one's trust betrayed. She had been quite right in her
assumption that her father had never betrayed that trust.
What she could never have imagined, not in a million
years, was that her mother should have been the one to
break that trust.

When Lorna returned to the conservatory to tell
Georgina that lunch was ready it was obvious from her
slightly brisk manner that the subject was now closed.
Through lunch their conversation revolved around the

girls, the hospital and Lorna's own activities in her village community.

It was after lunch while they were strolling in the garden counting the bulbs that were pushing through the rich dark earth that they heard the sound of the telephone ringing in the house. Lorna went to answer it, leaving Georgina in the garden.

Her mother's confession had shaken her and she knew she would need time to examine it, knowing instinctively that when she did so it would have a direct bearing on her own situation. She was just stooping beneath the bare branches of an old oak tree to pick a few snowdrops from the white drifts on the bank when she heard her mother's shout. She looked up sharply to see Lorna in the doorway, beckoning furiously to her.

Georgina straightened up with a sudden dread in her heart and, still clutching the snowdrops, sped across the lawn. 'What is it?' she asked.

'It's Jean Mitchell,' said Lorna. 'There's been an accident. It's Lauren, Georgina. She's been taken to the Shalbrooke. You're to go there immediately.'

CHAPTER TWELVE

'I NEED to get an urgent message to my husband. Yes, that's right. Andrew, Andrew Merrick. Dr Merrick. He'll be in a conference at the moment, but this really is extremely urgent. Thank you. Would you ask him to come to the phone, please? No, I'll wait.'

Georgina was making the call from Helen Turner's office, and it wasn't until the receptionist at the conference centre had gone to try to locate Andrew and Georgina had turned to look at Helen, who was watching her, that she realised her slip in referring to Andrew as her husband. Briefly she wondered what his reaction would be when he was told that his wife was wanting to speak to him. Then the thought was gone, the circumstances and events of the moment taking over again as she waited in an agony of suspense.

He came to the phone surprisingly quickly.

'Georgina, what is it?' He would know it was something crucial, that she would never have phoned him otherwise. It was such a relief to hear his voice after the traumatic events of the past hour that her legs threatened to give way beneath her.

'Andrew. . .' she took a deep breath '. . .it's Lauren. She's had a fall from a horse. I'm phoning from the Shalbrooke—'

'How is she. . .?'

'There's concussion, Andrew. She hasn't regained consciousness yet.'

'I'll come straight home.' He paused, then said, 'Georgina, how was she brought in?'

'Jean Mitchell had the sense to call an ambulance.'

'Thank God for that. I'll get the next train down.' His voice softened slightly. 'I'll be with you as soon as I can.' Georgina swallowed, trying to fight the knot of panic that had been in her stomach ever since Jean Mitchell had told her what had happened.

As she replaced the receiver she turned to Helen. 'He's coming straight home,' she said.

'It'll take him a few hours,' warned Helen.

'I don't care. I just want him here,' said Georgina simply.

'Where's Natasha?' asked Helen as she followed Georgina to the door.

'With my mother.'

'Good. I'll come up to Intensive Care with you.'

There was nothing she could do, nothing anyone could do, really, save wait for Lauren to regain consciousness. She lay on a bed in the ITU with an airway tube in her mouth. Her face was pale and her honey-blonde hair was spread across the pillow. Her eyes were closed, the long, dark lashes brushing her cheek.

As Georgina sat beside her, holding her hand and praying for her recovery, she was reminded of the young girl in the recent traffic accident—the one they had been unable to save—and she had to fight to banish the disturbing images from her mind.

The waiting for Andrew became unbearable, and when at last he arrived—in an impossibly short space of time, having been driven to Portsmouth by a sympathetic fellow delegate instead of having to wait for a train—it was not soon enough for Georgina. He strode into ITU his suit crumpled, his hair untidy, and deep lines of fatigue and strain etched on his features. As Georgina started up from the bedside she literally fell into his arms.

'Andrew. . .' Her voice was muffled as she buried her face against his chest. 'Oh, Andrew. . .'

'It's all right,' he whispered shakily against her hair, 'I'm here now.' He held her for a moment so close, so tightly, that she could hear his heart thumping, then gently he held her away and turned to the bed.

She saw his face crumple as he caught sight of Lauren. Her heart ached as she witnessed his struggle for control. As the doctor in him fought for supremacy over the father he leaned over and kissed Lauren's cheek, gently stroking her hair back from her forehead.

'Who has she seen?' he asked at last, swallowing furiously as he regained the use of his voice.

'Mr Cassidy and Robin Jarvis. 'It was Helen who replied, Helen who had been sitting quietly on the far side of the bed but who stood up now and faced Andrew and Georgina across the still form of their daughter. 'They said they would see you as soon as you arrived, Andrew. They will have the X-ray results.'

'Then I'd better go and see them.' He paused, still looking down at Lauren. 'Do you want to come with me, Georgina?'

She shook her head. 'No, Andrew. You go. I'll stay with Lauren. She may wake up. One of us should be here with her.'

'Very well.' He turned to go but hesitated and looked back at Lauren. 'Do we know exactly what happened?' he asked. 'She was wearing a hat, wasn't she?'

Georgina nodded. 'Yes, she was wearing her helmet. According to Jean Mitchell, something startled Dolly, the horse she was riding, and she reared, throwing Lauren to the ground. Whether her helmet wasn't secured properly or not, we don't know, but apparently it came off as she hit the ground and Jean thinks one of Dolly's hooves may have caught the side of Lauren's head.'

'Oh, God.' Andrew bowed his head and after a moment added, 'Was she conscious then?'

'Jean said no. She was knocked unconscious immediately and she hasn't regained it since.'

'I see.' Andrew looked devastated and Georgina's heart filled with dread. 'I'll be back soon.' Briefly he squeezed Georgina's hand and it was only then that she realised she'd been clinging to him ever since he'd arrived. Helplessly she let him go and watched as he walked from the ward.

Helen, who was off duty, sat with Georgina until Andrew returned. He was accompanied by a short, balding man with a yellow rosebud in the lapel of his immaculate grey suit. Georgina guessed that this was Fergus Cassidy who, she knew, was reknowned for his habitual daily rosebud. Irrelevantly she found herself wondering where he obtained them at this time of the year.

'Mrs Merrick.' He took her hand. 'We have decided,' he said, coming straight to the point, 'to wait and see if your daughter regains consciousness naturally. I'll be completely honest with you,' he went on, looking straight into her eyes, 'I'm not entirely happy with her X-rays and surgery may well become necessary, but I don't want us to rush into that without just cause. I propose, and your husband agrees with me—' he glanced at Andrew as he spoke '—that we let nature take its course through the night and review the situation again in the morning. Are you in agreement with that decision?' Calm grey eyes met hers.

'Yes,' she swallowed and nodded. 'Yes, of course.'

It was longest night of their lives. They kept their vigil seated not on either side of Lauren's bed but together, their hands clasped and their silent prayers as one for this dearly loved, first-born child.

Andrew left the ward once to phone Lorna and his own parents, returning with the mobile phone trolley so that they could both speak to a tearful Natasha who was unable to sleep.

Helen went home to tend to her father, returning shortly after midnight to offer quiet support.

Staff carried out necessary observations, procedures from which both Georgina and Andrew felt curiously detached—almost as if, despite their professional training, they had no knowledge of what was being done for their daughter.

A little before dawn, at the darkest hour, there came a flurry of activity from the staff, and quite suddenly Fergus Cassidy was back.

Georgina had no idea whether he had been there all night or whether he had been called in. She only knew that he was there, in control of what was happening. Andrew stood up and slipped quietly out of the ward to speak to the consultant and Georgina continued to sit with Lauren who, throughout the long night, had remained so still that at times they had feared the worst.

Briefly, sick with fatigue and worry, she rested her head on her arms and closed her eyes.

Images flashed through her mind. Lauren on the night she was born, the soft downy head cradled in the crook of her arm. Asleep in her cot, a single night-light burning... A toddler running across wet sand to the water's edge, her hair streaming behind her... A little girl's awe and excitement on the birth of her sister... Precious memories, indelibly imprinted on her mind...

She was in a meadow filled with flowers, large white marguerites scarlet poppies and cornflowers as blue as the sky. Andrew was there and so were the girls. They were laughing and flying a kite, which was strange because as far as Georgina could remember they had never owned a kite. The kite had a face—a dragon-like face—and a tail, a long, long tail that dived and swooped then streaked behind the kite as it soared up and up into the sky. . .higher and higher. . .

'Georgina.' Startled, she lifted her head. She wanted to stay in the meadow. They had all been together again there. They had been happy. Andrew was touching her arm. She must have drifted off for a moment. Staff surrounded the bed.

'What is it?' she said as reality returned and seized her. 'What's happened?' Her gaze flew to Lauren.

'It's all right,' said Andrew, taking her hands and drawing her gently to her feet. 'They are going to move her, Georgina—'

'Move her! Where to?' Her eyes widened with fear.

'To Southampton. . .the neurological unit. . .'

'No! Oh, no, not that.' Tears filled her eyes.

'They have to,' said Andrew. 'We don't have the facilities here. Fergus fears a blood clot. They have to operate—it's her only chance, Georgina.' His voice was harsh, raw with emotion.

Helplessly she stared at him, knowing every word he said was true.

'They are going to airlift her,' he went on.

'I want to go with her,' said Georgina.

'Of course,' Andrew replied.

'And you, Andrew. I want you with me.'

'Where else did you think I would be going?' he said huskily.

Once events were set in motion everything happened fast. To Georgina it was as if it was happening to someone else and she was an observer, someone on the outside looking in. The hospital ambulance took Lauren, herself, Andrew and a nurse through the grey dawn of the early morning to the helicopter that waited in the field behind the hospital, its rotor-blades still whirring. And it seemed that within no time at all they had taken off, had flown across the cold, grey waters of the Solent, landed at Southampton and Lauren was whipped away from them out of their sight to the operating theatre.

The waiting was agony yet somehow, because it was shared, because they were in it together and because of some peaceful, outside force it became bearable, and when at last the surgeon strode into the room and he was smiling, the relief was so intense it overwhelmed them both.

'I've removed the clot,' he said simply. 'I'm hopeful she will make a full recovery.'

She was still under the effect of the anaesthetic when they saw her but it was evident to them both that now, she merely slept, peacefully. They clung to each other as they watched her, weak with relief.

'You will wear the red dress, Mummy, won't you?' Natasha was lying on her stomach on Georgina's bed, watching her as she got ready to go out.

'No.' It was Lauren who answered, a fully recovered Lauren who was sitting beside her sister, also intently watching her mother. 'No,' she said again, 'Mum will wear the black dress tonight.'

Georgina met her elder daughter's gaze in the dressing table mirror. 'You are quite right, darling,' she said, 'I shall wear the black tonight.'

'Daddy likes the red best,' grumbled Natasha.

'He also likes the black,' said Lauren.

The girls were silent for a moment then Natasha said, 'It'll be nice having Helen looking after us tonight, seeing that Granny is away.'

'Did she mind?' asked Lauren.

'It was her idea,' Georgina replied. As the doorbell sounded she said, 'Here she is now. Run downstairs and let her in.' As the girls scrambled from the bed and clattered down the stairs Georgina stared at her own reflection in the mirror, critically summing up what she saw. The black dress still looked good while her hair, which she'd brushed until it gleamed, she wore loose just the way he liked it. Leaning forward, she carefully scutinised her face. There were tiny fine lines of tension around her eyes which surely were new but which, under the circumstances, she thought with a sigh, were hardly surprising.

Straightening up, she picked up her glass perfume bottle and sprayed her throat and wrists with the light fragrance she always wore, the one she'd made her own. With a deep breath and a final glance round the room she made her way down the stairs.

Helen was in the sitting-room, talking to the girls, but she looked up as Georgina came into the room. 'Hello,' she said, 'you look nice.'

'Thanks. . .' Georgina smiled, then said, 'This is very good of you, you know.'

'Not at all. Is Andrew picking you up?'

Georgina nodded, and as they all heard the sound of a car outside she said, 'Here he is now by the sounds of it.' And suddenly she knew the feelings she had been fighting all the time she had been getting ready were those of nervousness. She was as apprehensive as any teenager getting ready for her first date, felt, in fact, very much as she had done all those years ago when Andrew had met her from the café, they'd walked on the beach and he'd bought her an ice cream, before walking her to the bus stop.

And here he was again, only this time the jeans and T-shirt had been replaced by a dark suit and a crisp white shirt, which when she first caught sight of him caused her heart to skip a beat, but the smile was the same, that same lazy, sexy smile that had captivated her then and had done so ever since.

He spoke briefly to Helen, laughed teasingly with the

girls, but that was all. Tonight was theirs. Theirs alone.

For Helen, watching them as they left the cottage, the certainty was almost as strong as it was for Georgina. She had recognised their need to spend time alone together, following the trauma of Lauren's accident, and had consequently offered to look after the girls for the evening. The fact that it had involved all kinds of organisation in her own household in arranging for help with her father was for Helen neither here nor there. It was all worth it to see Georgina and Andrew looking happy again.

'Didn't Mum look lovely?' sighed Lauren as Helen closed the front door.

'Yes,' Helen agreed, 'she certainly did.'

'Daddy looked nice, too,' said Natasha as she set out the Monopoly board. When the others agreed she went on, 'Really, I would like to have gone with them.'

'Not tonight,' said Helen as she sat down at the table and began sorting out the banknotes.

'Why not?' Natasha demanded.

Looking up, Helen met Lauren's gaze across the table.

'Because—' it was Lauren who answered '—tonight is special.'

'Why is it special?' Natasha persisted.

'Because tonight I think Dad will ask Mum to marry him,' Lauren replied.

'Well, I think that's silly,' said Natasha leaning over the table and carefully choosing the top hat as her marker.

'Why do you think it's silly?' Helen turned to look at her, wondering for the moment if she'd been mistaken in her assumption that these two girls had wanted a reconciliation as much as she had.

'It just is,' said Natasha, vigorously shaking the dice. 'After all, they were married anyway—weren't they?

You can't get married again.' With a flourish she tossed the dice across the board.

'I thought it appropriate that we should come here— where we celebrated our last anniversary together.' Leaning across the table, Andrew stretched out his hand and covered Georgina's where it lay on the white tablecloth. They had finished their meal and lingered now over coffee in the soft glow of candlelight.

'A lot has happened since then, Andrew,' she replied quietly.

'I agree,' he nodded, 'and most of it has been pretty awful. . .and yet. . .'

'Yet what?'

'I don't know.' He hesitated. 'Somehow I seem to have found out a lot about myself recently, especially in the last couple of weeks. . .somehow what happened to Lauren helped to get a lot of things into perspective.'

Slowly Georgina nodded. 'Yes. . .for me, too, I think.'

They were silent for a moment, each wrapped in their own thoughts and memories, oblivious to the other diners around them. Slowly, carefully, Andrew said, 'I bitterly regretted our divorce, Georgina, and the events that led up to it, but I think you already know that. . .'

He paused, as if struggling to find the right words, and quite unexpectedly she found herself wanting to help him but not quite knowing how, and at the same time knowing that what he was trying to say had to be said.

At last he seemed able to continue. 'What the events of the last weeks have shown me,' he said, 'is just how deep the bonds of marriage and of having a family really go. Do you. . .?' He hesitated again. 'Georgina, do you think there may be a chance we could try again?'

She was silent for a long moment, reflecting, then she lifted her head and looked at Andrew across the candle-lit table. She said, 'I'll be completely honest with you,

Andrew, if you'd asked me that question a couple of weeks ago I would still have been wary. . .uncertain if we could make a go of it again. I would have said we still had a lot of talking, explaining and reasoning to do. . .'

'But now. . .?' He stared at her and there was no mistaking the hope that flickered in his dark eyes.

'Now.' She paused and began making patterns on the tablecloth with her thumb nail. 'Now, I think I'm inclined to say that I've come to realise just how short life really is. . .of how anyone is capable of making a mistake and of how these things are usually not all the fault of just one person. I've also realised how important it is to forgive. But. . .' she swallowed. . .more than all of that, I also have truly, and probably for the first time, understood what love really is, what it's all about. . .'

Looking up, she met his gaze again, squarely, with no pretence. 'I love you, Andrew,' she said simply. 'I always have, from that very first moment when you walked into that café. . .and I guess I always will. . . You are my husband and you are the father of my children. . .'

'If only you knew how much I've longed to hear you say that.' His voice, suddenly breaking into hers, was husky with emotion.

'I'm not pretending it will all be plain sailing and that we don't still have a lot of talking to do,' she went on. 'But I feel we owe it to each other and to the girls to give it another try.'

They sat on, talking, while the candles burnt down. Andrew told her how he had longed to make a move before but of how he had been afraid of rushing her, of her reaction. They talked of the night he had spent at the cottage and of how spontaneous their love-making had been the following morning. 'As natural as breathing, really,' he said with a sheepish smile, and she had been forced to agree. They talked of her career and of how

Andrew had finally come to understand how important it was to her.

'But not at the expense of being a mother,' she added. 'That will always take priority.'

'I think you've more than proved that,' he said.

There was no dance band that night as there had been on their anniversary night, just a solitary man who played haunting melodies on a grand piano in the shadows beyond the edges of the small dance floor.

The waiter brought them fresh coffee then retreated, leaving them alone as if recognising and respecting their need for solitude.

Other couples took to the floor, drifting in the flickering candlelight, and still they talked, putting right so much of what had been wrong between them, until at last Andrew rose to his feet, took her hand, drew her up and into his arms and they, too, joined the few couples left on the floor.

For a long time they swayed gently to the music, their cheeks touching, her arms entwined around his neck. Neither of them spoke but both were aware of the other's growing arousal, each anticipating what would now inevitably follow.

'I love you, Georgina,' he whispered at last. 'I love you so very much. . . You mean the whole world to me. . . I only wish there was a way I could show you how much.'

Drawing slightly away from him, she looked up into his face and—feeling quite heady from a mixture of the wine, the atmosphere and the renewal of their love for each other—she said, 'There just might just be a way, you know. . .there just might be.'

'Tell me,' he murmured, bending his head and at the same time running his hands down her back, moulding her hips and her waist and pressing her even closer against him until her body seems to melt into his own.

'I understand,' she said with a little shudder of pure

pleasure, a touch of mischief entering her eyes, 'I understand, from what I've been told, that Venice can be rather nice at this time of the year. Maybe we should find out for ourselves.'

She sensed his surprise that she should be suggesting this so soon, felt the tremor that went through him. 'Maybe we should, Mrs Merrick,' he said and then, delighted laughter catching his throat, he added, 'maybe we should at that.'

The next *Matchmaker* story is in April.
Find out then how Helen manages
to bring Kate and Jonathan together in
FROM THIS DAY FORWARD

MILLS & BOON®

Medical Romance™

COMING NEXT MONTH

THAT FOREVER FEELING by Caroline Anderson

'It was only a kiss,' Holly told Dan. It may have started with a kiss but this was the beginning of something much, much more.

MAKING BABIES by Lilian Darcy

Book one (of two)

Nicole's rules were clear—a good time and no commitment. There was only one problem—Richard thought a good time meant *bedtime*!

SUNSHINE REMEDY by Mary Hawkins

Kids and Kisses

Daniel had his daughter to consider. The last thing he needed was a relationship with career-minded Cindy, but he was only too happy to be proved wrong.

SURROGATE FATHER by Rebecca Lang

Marcus thought he was the perfect candidate to help Lisa look after her baby. And as for Lisa, she thought Marcus was exactly that—*perfect!*

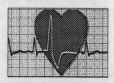

Available from WH Smith, John Menzies, Volume One, Forbuoys, Martins, Tesco, Asda and other paperback stockists.

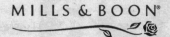

4 FREE

books and a surprise gift!

We would like to take this opportunity to thank you for reading this Mills & Boon® book by offering you the chance to take FOUR more specially selected titles from the Medical Romance™ series absolutely FREE! We're also making this offer to introduce you to the benefits of the Reader Service™—

★ FREE home delivery
★ FREE gifts and competitions
★ FREE monthly newsletter
★ Books available before they're in the shops
★ Exclusive Reader Service discounts

Accepting these FREE books and gift places you under no obligation to buy, you may cancel at any time, even after receiving your free shipment. Simply complete your details below and return the entire page to the address below. *You don't even need a stamp!*

YES! Please send me 4 free Medical Romance books and a surprise gift. I understand that unless you hear from me, I will receive 4 superb new titles every month for just £2.20 each, postage and packing free. I am under no obligation to purchase any books and may cancel my subscription at any time. The free books and gift will be mine to keep in any case.

M8XE

Ms/Mrs/Miss/Mr.................................Initials ....
BLOCK CAPITALS PLEASE

Surname ....

Address ....

....

....Postcode.................................

Send this whole page to:
THE READER SERVICE, FREEPOST, CROYDON, CR9 3WZ
(Eire readers please send coupon to: P.O. BOX 4546, DUBLIN 24.)